The Boxcar Children are on a surprise mission!

Trudy smiled. She took a business card out of her bag and handed it to the children. "Contact me if you have any trouble. We've arranged all your travel for you," she said as she pushed herself up and out of her chair with her crutches. As she stepped off the train, she called, "Good luck! Be careful!"

Benny felt a strange sensation beneath his feet. Watch barked. "The floor is rumbling!" he cried. "The train is moving!"

"It can't be!" Violet said, running over to look out the window. She was shocked to see that Benny was right. The train was moving forward, picking up speed...

THE BOXCAR CHILDREN MYSTERIES

BOXCAR CHILDREN®

CREATED BY
GERTRUDE CHANDLER WARNER

JOURNEY ON A RUNAWAY TRAIN

STORY BY
DEE GARRETSON AND JM LEE

ILLUSTRATED BY
ANTHONY VanARSDALE

ALBERT WHITMAN & COMPANY
CHICAGO, ILLINOIS

Contents

CHAPTER 1

An Exciting Thing About to Happen

The tinkling of little bells woke Jessie Alden up. As she lay in her bed, she wondered whether she had dreamed the nice noises. She looked over to the window. It was very early in the morning. Her room was just beginning to brighten. The curtains billowed as a breeze blew through them. The bells sounded again and then Jessie remembered. She and her ten-year-old sister, Violet, had hung a mobile in Jessie's room the night before.

Violet's latest art project was mobile making. For Jessie's mobile, she had cut out pictures of amazing sites from all over the world. The pictures were glued to cardboard and then tied to strings hanging from a wire frame. Violet had added little silver bells on strings to hang among the pictures. She said she hoped her mobile would give Jessie dreams of all the places she might go someday.

Jessie listened to the bells, thinking it was almost like they were signaling her to get up. Soft footsteps sounded in the hallway as if someone was trying not to be heard. Jumping out of bed, Jessie darted over to her door and opened it. Her fourteen-year-old brother, Henry, and Watch, their dog, were just heading down the stairs. Violet and six-year-old Benny opened their own doors.

Jessie noticed no one looked sleepy. "Why are we all so awake?" she whispered.

"I was too excited to sleep late, but I don't know why," Benny said.

"I felt the same way, like something exciting was going to happen and I didn't want to miss it," Violet added.

"That's strange," Henry said. "I felt the same way."

Watch wagged his tail as if he were agreeing with them.

They stood there for a moment until Violet

asked, "What do we do now? It's really early."

"First, we should go downstairs so we won't wake anyone else up," Jessie said. They went down to the kitchen. Henry filled up Watch's bowl with dog food. Watch wolfed it down.

"I'm just as hungry as Watch," Benny said. "What time is breakfast?"

"Not for a while," Jessie said. "Mrs. McGregor thought we would sleep late since it's the first day of spring break." Mrs. McGregor was the Aldens' housekeeper.

"How long is a while?" Benny asked. "However long it is, I don't think I can wait."

"I have an idea," Violet said. "Since it's finally stopped raining, it would be nice to go outside. Let's make our own breakfast and take it out to the boxcar to eat." The Aldens had their very own boxcar in their backyard. It was a special place for them. After their parents died, they had been scared to go live at their grandfather's house. Fearing he would be mean, the children had run away and found an old boxcar in the woods. They lived there until their grandfather found them. He was not mean at all, and he even arranged for the boxcar to be brought to his yard.

"I like Violet's idea." Benny jumped up and down. "We can have a breakfast picnic!"

Jessie smiled at Benny's excitement. "We have some blueberry muffins I made and there are some bananas. That would be a good breakfast."

"Perfect," Henry said.

"Violet, will you carry the muffins?" Jessie asked. "I'll take the plates and the bananas. Henry can carry the glasses. Benny, that means you are in charge of the juice."

They took everything out to the boxcar, squishing their way across the wet backyard.

"There is something about this morning that feels so different," Violet said as they laid out their breakfast. Rain began to ping on the roof of the boxcar.

"Except the rain." Henry sighed.

"At least the rain makes the air smell good," Violet said.

"I don't know if I've ever heard so many birds chirping this early in the spring," Jessie said. "Listen."

An Exciting Thing About to Happen

It did seem as if their yard was filled with birds. The children were quiet as they ate their breakfast, enjoying the sound of the birds.

"Sometimes I wish this boxcar was still attached to a train," Benny said when they were finished. "And that we were going someplace right now."

"I wish we could have an adventure this week," Jessie said. "We haven't had any mysteries to solve recently, and I'm ready for one. Anyone heard of any mysteries that need solving?"

"No," Henry said glumly. "I've even asked around. No one has lost anything or seen any strange things lately."

"It's like all the mysteries have been solved," Violet said, just as glumly as Henry.

"Don't be sad." Benny looked around at his brother and sisters. "It's still the first day of spring break. Let's play a game. Everybody close your eyes and imagine where you'd like the boxcar to go."

"There are so many places. It is hard to"—a rumbling noise drowned out the rest of Violet's sentence.

"Do you hear that?" Benny opened his eyes. "Is the train moving?"

Henry got up and went to the door of the boxcar. "No, it's thunder. Looks like it's going to storm again."

"Let's get inside before the rain gets too heavy," Jessie said. They collected the picnic supplies and got ready to run for the back door. Watch jumped out of the boxcar and then stopped, his ears perking up. He gave a bark and then dashed toward the front of the house. As he disappeared around the corner, he began to bark again.

"He's going to wake up the neighbors," Jessie said.

"Watch!" Henry called.

Watch didn't come back. He kept barking.

"We'd better go see what he's doing," Benny said.

The four of them ran around the house to the front yard. Violet was in the lead, but when she got to the front yard, she skidded to a stop on the wet grass. The others nearly ran into her. "There's someone on our front porch," she said.

They could see a man standing on the top of

the steps looking at Watch. Watch was on the walkway at the bottom of the steps looking back at the man.

He was an older man, about Grandfather's age. He was very small with a wrinkly face and silvery gray hair that stuck out from underneath a purple cap.

When the man saw the Aldens, he tipped his cap at them and smiled. Violet noticed the cap matched the purple bow tie he wore. He had a silver hoop earring in one ear and one front tooth capped in silver.

"Good morning, children," he said. "Lovely day, isn't it?"

Jessie wasn't so sure such a gray rainy day could be called lovely, but the man didn't even seem to notice he was all wet.

"Sorry about our dog," Henry said to the man. "Watch won't hurt you. He just barks at strangers sometimes."

"That's all right," the man replied. "I understand. Back when I was a pirate, I learned you can't trust everyone. Sometimes you need to bark at people just to let them know you are watching them."

Benny's eyes opened wide. "You were a pirate?"

The man's smile grew. "Some people called me that a long time ago. Today I'm just passing out flyers. I've put one in your door." He winked at them and then tipped his cap again. "Good day to you."

He came down the steps and patted Watch on the head as he walked by. The dog wagged his tail. The Aldens watched as the man then strolled down the sidewalk away from them. Right before he turned the corner and disappeared from the Aldens' sight, he jumped up and clicked his heels together.

"That was an interesting man," Jessie said. "Maybe he was the exciting thing we thought would happen today."

"He was interesting, but now he's gone," Henry said. "That's not very exciting."

"I wonder why he left us a flyer." Violet ran up the steps and pulled out a piece of paper that had been stuck between the door and the frame. She held it up for the others to see.

The flyer had an image of an old storage trunk on the top and the words "Reddimus Curiosities Antique Dealers" beneath.

Benny pointed to the next line. "I can read the first part. It says *We make house calls*. I can't read a couple of the other words in the rest of the sentence."

Violet read it for him. "It says *We make house calls to appraise all your curiosities*."

"I don't understand," Benny said. "What does appraise mean?"

"It means to look at something and decide how much it is worth," Henry told him. "This antique dealer comes around to people's houses to see if they have valuable old things they might want to sell. A curiosity is an interesting or rare item."

"That old trunk on the flyer looks exactly like the one we have in the study. So is our trunk a curiosity?" Benny asked.

"I guess it could be," Violet replied. "I never think about our trunk because it's always been there."

"Mrs. McGregor thinks about it," Jessie said. "She doesn't like it because it takes up so much room."

Mrs. McGregor opened the front door just then. "I thought I heard voices. What are you children doing out here on the porch?"

An Exciting Thing About to Happen

Jessie explained about the picnic and the man and the flyer as they went inside. "Did you let the man in?" Mrs. McGregor asked. "The floor is all wet."

Grandfather came out of the kitchen carrying a cup of coffee. "I've been looking for you, Mrs. McGregor. I let the fellow inside. He said he had an appointment with you to talk about cleaning the gutters."

"I didn't have an appointment with anyone!" Mrs. McGregor frowned. "Why would he say that?"

"The flyer doesn't have anything on it about gutters." Jessie handed it to Grandfather.

"Look!" Violet pointed at the floor. Wet footprints led down the hallway. They faded away about halfway down.

"Do you think he was trying to steal something?" Benny cried.

"Should we call the police?" Mrs. McGregor asked.

"Let's not get ahead of ourselves," Grandfather said. "I don't think anyone from Reddimus would steal something from us."

"Do you know about that business, Grandfather?" Henry asked.

"I've heard of them," Grandfather said. "They have a good reputation."

"Why don't we see if anything is missing?" Henry said.

Jessie glanced around the hallway. "Nothing looks to be missing here. Why don't we check the other rooms?" The children split up, each taking a room on the first floor.

"I need another cup of coffee," Grandfather said. "Mrs. McGregor, you look like you need one too. We'll let the children search, but I don't think they are going to find anything missing."

They had only been searching for a few seconds when they heard Benny yell, "The trunk!" The children raced into the study. Benny stood there pointing at the trunk.

Jessie was puzzled. "Why did you yell, Benny? The trunk is right in front of us. It's not missing."

"The trunk has been moved!" he said. "It's not all the way up against the wall anymore."

Mrs. McGregor and Grandfather came in.

An Exciting Thing About to Happen

Mrs. McGregor said, "That old thing! I wish someone would steal it. It takes up too much room and it's hard to dust. And it's not a proper storage place for important papers. Everything gets all jumbled inside."

"But it's part of the house," Grandfather said. "I can remember it here when I was a little boy, so that means it's very old. I suppose I should move our passports somewhere else though."

"I hope someone didn't steal those," Henry said.

"I'll check." Jessie lifted the lid. "They're here," she said, relieved at the sight of the documents.

"What's that?" Benny pointed at something wrapped in silver tissue paper in one corner of the trunk.

"I don't know," Grandfather said.

Violet took the object out and unwrapped it carefully. Everyone crowded around to see. Inside the bundle was a tiny painted ceramic turtle. It had a black and orange design on its back.

"I don't remember ever seeing that before." Grandfather frowned. "Do you, Mrs. McGregor?"

"No, never." The housekeeper shook her head.

"That's strange. May I see the turtle, Violet?" Grandfather's voice had become very serious. Violet handed it to him. "I need to make a phone call in private," he said. "Why don't you all get dressed and then come back down." He motioned for them to go out in the hall. As soon as they were out of the room, he shut the door so he was in the study by himself.

Henry was surprised at the sudden change in Grandfather. "Let's do what Grandfather wants," he said. "I think we may have a mystery to solve after all."

The Turtle and the Truck

When the children were dressed they came back downstairs, then Grandfather opened the door to the study and called them in. "I've changed my mind," he said. "Mrs. McGregor is right. We need a file cabinet for important papers. I never liked that trunk and I don't like that turtle. Jessie, you can call the place on the flyer and ask them to get someone over here to appraise it."

"Are you sure?" Mrs. McGregor asked. "It has been here a long time. It's not that difficult to dust."

"And it fits in with all the other old things in the study," Violet said. "Like the old telephone and the typewriter in here."

"I've decided," Grandfather insisted. "We're getting rid of it."

"I'll call," Jessie said. But she couldn't help but wonder—why had Grandfather changed his mind so quickly?

Jessie dialed the number. Someone answered the phone on the first ring. A man's raspy voice said, "Reddimus Curiosities. We're curious about everything." Jessie explained about the trunk.

"That sounds like something we might find very interesting," the man said. "We'll be over in..." he paused and then added, "seven minutes." He hung up the phone before she could say anything in reply.

Jessie put down the phone. "They're interested. Someone will be over in...er, seven minutes."

"Seven minutes? How do they know that's how long it will take them?" Henry asked.

Jessie shrugged. "I don't know. That's what the man told me."

Henry looked at his watch. When seven minutes were up and the doorbell hadn't rung, he said, "So they didn't really know how long it would take them."

The Turtle and the Truck

Benny ran to the window to look out. "There is a truck out front!" he cried.

"That's strange," Jessie said as she went to the door and opened it. "I didn't hear a truck pull up."

A big old white truck was parked outside. The words *Reddimus Curiosities* were painted in purple letters on the truck's side. There was also a logo that consisted of a fancy *R* inside a circle made up of swirls. An image of an owl was placed so it looked like it was sitting on top of the letter. A man got out and hurried up the Aldens' steps. He was dressed in a very formal black suit with a white shirt and a purple flower in the buttonhole of his coat. He had on a purple bow tie just like the one on the man who had delivered the flyer.

Jessie whispered to Violet, "He's very dressed up to be driving a truck."

Violet whispered back, "He's a little scary looking, or else he's not feeling well. He's very pale."

Benny took a step away from the window. "He looks like a vampire!"

Henry put his hand on Benny's shoulder. "Benny, vampires aren't real. You know that."

"If they were real, they'd look like him," Benny said.

Grandfather opened the door. The man handed him a business card but didn't speak. Jessie caught a glimpse of it. It had the same R in a circle that the truck had on it and a few words. She didn't get a good enough look to read them.

Grandfather looked at the card and said, "Mr. Ganert, thank you for coming so promptly." He introduced the children.

Mr. Ganert shook all their hands and then said in a low voice, "Tell me about the man who left the flyer." His words came out crackly and hoarse as if he didn't speak much. "We don't have anyone in the neighborhood handing out flyers."

Jessie described him. "Did I forget anything?" she asked the rest of them.

"You forgot the part about how he had been a pirate," Benny said.

"He did say that," Jessie told Mr. Ganert. "He was probably just joking around."

Mr. Ganert frowned. "Yes. I don't believe we have any former pirates working for us. This is all very odd. I'd like to see the trunk and the turtle now, if possible."

They took him into the study. He examined the trunk and the turtle very carefully. When he was done, he said, "I need to buy both items. I'll give you five hundred dollars for the two."

Grandfather nodded. "They're all yours."

The man pulled a checkbook and a pen out of his coat pocket. He wrote a check and handed it to Grandfather. "I want to pick these up as soon as possible. I'll come back in a few hours with a helper to collect them. You will need to unload the contents you want to save. We'll take anything you don't want."

"That's fine with me," Grandfather said. He turned to the children. "Can you unload the trunk? I've got a meeting I need to get to."

"We can do it," Jessie said. "We'll get started right away." She was surprised Grandfather was going out. He wasn't wearing a suit as he usually did for work meetings.

Grandfather smiled. "I'll show Mr. Ganert out since I need to leave if I'm going to get to my meeting on time."

Mr. Ganert shook all their hands again and said, "Until we meet again."

As soon as they were gone, Violet wiped her hand on her shirt. "Ugh. His hand was cold and sweaty at the same time."

"He acted like he didn't want to be here," Jessie said.

Benny looked out the window to make sure Mr. Ganert was gone. "I hope we don't have to meet him again. I still think he might be a vampire."

Mrs. McGregor said, "Let's not worry about him any longer. I have a box in the basement I can give you for the papers in until we get a file cabinet. Benny, why don't you come down with me and you can carry it back up."

"Okay," Benny agreed and followed Mrs. McGregor out of the room.

Jessie opened the lid of the trunk again and peered in. "The stack on the right is old magazines. I don't know why we saved those."

Violet picked up one and leafed through it. "I don't either. They aren't even ones we could cut up for the pictures." She put it back in the trunk.

"I'd like to look at that turtle again before it's taken away."

"Me too," Benny said as he came in carrying a box. "I really like it."

"I just don't understand how it got here," Henry said. "Last year I went all through the trunk when I was looking for some old photographs and I know it wasn't there then."

Violet picked the turtle up and then turned it over. "Sometimes potters or pottery makers put their names on the bottom of the work. Look. Here's something." On the underside of the turtle were the letters *I K A C O M A*.

"That must be the name of the artist," Jessie said.

Violet turned it back over and looked at the design on its back again. "This might be a Native American design. I saw a book on famous Native American potters at the pottery studio when I took a class there. The book was full of pictures of their beautiful pottery. The design on this turtle looks like some of the pictures."

"There are hundreds of Native American

nations," Henry said. "That doesn't narrow it down much."

"Yes, I know," Violet said. "And my teacher said not every nation has a tradition of making pottery. The ones that do each have their own designs, and individual artists have their own styles too. We'd have to do a lot more research."

"Could Ikacoma be the name of a Native American nation?" Jessie asked.

"Maybe," Violet said.

Jessie put a stack of their old artwork in the box. "I'll go get my laptop and we can research it. It will just take a minute, and then we can finish the trunk."

When she had brought the laptop down and turned it on, she typed in *Ikacoma*. "Nothing is coming up under that word. No person and no Native American nation."

"The library has a whole section of books on art," Violet said. "We could look there."

"We can go after we finish with the trunk," Henry said.

"We shouldn't take the turtle with us," Violet said. "It really doesn't belong to us anymore since Mr. Ganert gave Grandfather the check for it. What if we dropped it and broke it?"

Henry took his cell phone out of his pocket. "We can leave it here. I'll take some pictures of it."

The telephone on the desk rang just as Henry finished photographing the turtle. Henry answered it. He listened and then said, "We'll be right there." Hanging up the phone, he said, "There's an emergency at Storytown Books. The roof is leaking and a lot of rain is coming in. They're calling all the regular volunteers to see if we can come in to move the books before they get ruined."

"That's terrible," Violet said. "Their big sale to raise money for the library was supposed to start tomorrow."

"You all go," Jessie said. "I'll finish the trunk. We don't all need to do it, and when I'm done, I'll come help at the bookstore."

Violet picked the turtle up. "I'm going to wrap it back up. It would be awful if it broke."

"You can put it on top of the magazines," Jessie said. "I'm done with that part."

Once the turtle was back in the trunk, Violet hurried to catch up with Benny and Henry, who were putting on their coats and rain boots.

"Are you sure you don't want help, Jessie?" Henry asked.

"No, this is really a one-person job. I'll be done soon." She went back to work as soon as Henry, Violet, and Benny were out the door.

As she picked up a pile of postcards, Watch put

his front paws on the side of the trunk and looked in. He crouched down as if he were ready to leap up into it.

"No, Watch, you can't get in there," Jessie said, grabbing his collar. He whined but obeyed, sitting down next to her and sniffing the postcards.

"I bet you smell all the places these have been." she said. They were postcards the Aldens had mailed to Mrs. McGregor on their travels. "We'll definitely save these." Jessie put them in the box. "I hope we get to send more soon."

The phone rang again. Jessie picked it up and said hello.

"Is this Jessie?" A woman asked in a whispered voice.

"Yes," Jessie replied. She couldn't recognize the voice.

"This is Mrs. Jamison. I've lost my voice and I need your help." Mrs. Jamison was their friend who lived around the corner. The Aldens often did yard work for her. "Mittens has gotten out, and it's raining, and I'm so worried about him. I got a call that a black and white cat who looked like him was spotted in the park. I hate to ask you to go out in the rain, but I've been very ill and I don't know who else to call."

"I'm sure I can find him," Jessie said. "I'll go to the park right away."

"Thank you. Thank you! I don't know what I'd do without you." The woman hung up the phone before Jessie could say goodbye.

Jessie was about to go get her coat when she saw Watch eying the trunk again. "You aren't going to get in there while I'm gone," she told the dog as she shut the lid.

She searched the park for a long time but couldn't find the cat. Hoping he had gone home, she hurried to Mrs. Jamison's house. She rang the doorbell and Mrs. Jamison opened the door.

"Jessie, what a nice surprise," Mrs. Jamison said in a normal voice. She didn't sound or look ill at all. "Won't you come in?"

"Did Mittens come home?" Jessie asked. "I couldn't find him in the park."

"In the park? What would he be doing there? He's been asleep all morning on his favorite chair."

The Turtle and the Truck

Jessie was very confused. She explained about the phone call.

"That wasn't me," Mrs. Jamison said. "It sounds like someone was playing a mean trick on you. How terrible! And now you are all wet. Won't you come in for some hot chocolate?"

"No thank you," Jessie said. "I have another place I need to be."

As she walked home, Jessie wondered if the others would still need her help at the bookstore. It had taken her so long at the park, she thought the bookstore problem might already be solved.

When she turned the corner to the Alden's street, she was surprised to see the Reddimus Curiosities truck was in front of their house. A man began to close the back gate on the truck. Jessie could see the trunk inside it. "No, wait!" Jessie yelled. The man didn't hear her. He climbed into the truck and drove off.

"Oh, no!" She ran as fast as she could but quickly realized she was not going to be able to catch it, at least not on foot. She stopped for a moment and took a deep breath. Then she raced to the garage and grabbed her bike and jumped on.

She saw the truck just as it turned the corner onto another side street. Jessie followed, braking just enough to make the tight turn. *Please stop!* her mind screamed as she kept her eyes on the truck and tried to get closer.

Finally, the truck came to a stop at a light a block away. Jessie hoped she could reach it in time. But the driver kept revving the engine and inching the vehicle forward. Jessie pedaled faster. *Almost there*, she thought.

When she was about ten feet behind the truck, the light changed and the truck sped through the intersection. Jessie sped up too, but the truck was too fast for her. She fell farther behind, hoping for another stoplight. Instead, the truck turned onto a very busy road and disappeared from her sight.

"No!" Jessie cried out loud. There was nothing she could do now except turn back and go home.

Curious about Reddimus Curiosities

Jessie was upset at herself for not telling Mrs. McGregor the trunk wasn't ready. What would they do now?

Her brothers and sister were already home when she went into the house.

"It was a trick!" Benny cried when he saw her. "There was no leak at the bookstore. We walked all the way there, and everything was fine!"

"Yes," Henry said. "I didn't recognize the voice on the phone. He wasn't speaking very loudly, but I just thought it was a bad connection. We can't figure it out."

"What's wrong, Jessie?" Violet asked. "You look upset."

"Someone played a trick on me too." She explained about Mittens and the Reddimus truck. "The trunk is gone and I hadn't finished unloading it."

"It sounds like someone wanted us out of the house," Henry said. "But I don't understand why."

"I don't either." Jessie grew more upset. "The worst part of this is that our passports are gone. I hadn't put them in the box yet."

"Maybe they took them out for us," Violet said.

"I'll go look." Benny ran into the study. After a moment he called, "I think you should come in here."

They hurried into the study. "Look," Benny said, pointing at the desk. "The turtle is still here."

"That can't be," Jessie said. "The turtle was in the trunk when I left and the lid was shut."

"Somehow it got back out." Henry picked it up. "There is something very strange going on."

Jessie looked at the turtle, amazed it was still in the house. "We need to ask Mrs. McGregor what happened," she said. "Maybe Mrs. McGregor took the passports before the men loaded the trunk."

The children ran into the kitchen and told the housekeeper what had happened.

Curious about Reddimus Curiosities

"Oh dear. I had no idea you hadn't finished going through the trunk, Jessie," Mrs. McGregor said. "I saw some papers in the box, so I thought you were finished."

"What about the turtle?" Benny asked. "How did it get back out of the trunk?"

"I don't know. I didn't take it out. I didn't see either of the two men take it out." Mrs. McGregor paused and then said, "There was something odd that happened. After I let them in and they started to move the trunk, the telephone rang. I couldn't reach the telephone on Mr. Alden's desk because the men and the trunk were in the way. I went into the kitchen to answer it, but there was no one there. When I came back, they already had the trunk out on the porch."

"So one of them had time to take the turtle out of the trunk without you seeing it," Henry said.

Mrs. McGregor nodded her head. "If they were quick about it, they could have."

"I'm worried about our passports," Jessie said. "We need to call Mr. Ganert right away. But I can't remember the telephone number of Reddimus Curiosities."

"I saw Grandfather put the business card down on the hall table," Violet said. "It will be on there. I'll go get it."

She brought the card into the kitchen. "We've got a problem. There is no phone number on it. No address either. The only things on it are the words *Reddimus Curiosities* and a couple of words I don't know how to pronounce." She sounded them out. "*Ar-te per-en-net.* I don't know what those words mean."

"Could I see the card?" Jessie asked. Violet handed it to her. Jessie looked at the unfamiliar words. "I don't know them either. I don't think *arte* or *perennet* are English words."

"Even if we knew what they meant, it wouldn't help us get in touch with Mr. Ganert," Henry said.

"I see something written on the back," Benny said.

Jessie turned the card over. "More odd words. *Confert Latinum.*"

Henry looked over Jessie's shoulder. "*Latinum*? That sounds like Latin. Maybe all those words are in Latin."

Curious about Reddimus Curiosities

"What's Latin?" Benny asked.

"It's an old language," Henry explained. "People still study it today. I'll take it in school next year."

"Even if we figure out how to translate the words, we still won't have a phone number," Violet said.

"Why don't you just look in the telephone book?" Benny suggested.

Henry laughed. "Smart, Benny. We should have thought of that. High five!" Henry held up his hand and Benny jumped up to slap it.

The children took the turtle back into the study. Henry pulled the telephone book out of the drawer in Grandfather's desk and leafed through it until he got to the R's. Running his finger down the page he read off a list of businesses beginning with RE. "There isn't a Reddimus Curiosities here. I don't understand why a business wouldn't be listed in the telephone book."

"What about the flyer?" Violet asked. "That's how Jessie got the number in the first place."

Jessie thought for a moment. "I think Grandfather

had it last." They searched everywhere but couldn't find it. Violet asked Mrs. McGregor, but the housekeeper hadn't seen it either.

Henry snapped his fingers. "I know. The man was delivering flyers all over the neighborhood. We can get the number off one of the neighbor's flyers."

"That's a good idea," Violet said. The children rang doorbells up and down the street. None of the neighbors on the street had received a flyer. As the Aldens walked back to the house, they discussed the problem.

"So why would that man deliver a flyer just to us?" Jessie wondered aloud. "It's almost like they knew the trunk was here and wanted to convince us to sell it to them."

"Do you think they wanted to steal our passports?" Benny asked.

"No," Henry said. "They wouldn't know the passports were in the trunk in the first place, and once they bought the trunk, they couldn't know Jessie wouldn't have time to take the passports out."

"Except Jessie did get the mysterious phone

call," Violet reminded them.

They reached their house, walking up the steps to the porch. "What about the phone history on the telephone?" Jessie suggested. "It should have the last number we called."

Henry shook his head as he opened the door. "Don't you remember? We used Grandfather's old-fashioned dial phone in the study. That doesn't have a phone history on it, and the calls don't show up on the other phones."

"Maybe Mr. Ganert will come back when he finds the turtle isn't in the trunk," Benny said. He didn't say it out loud but he was glad the turtle had been left behind. He really, really liked it.

Jessie couldn't stop worrying about the passports. "I hope so," she said, "but we should tell Grandfather."

When Grandfather came home and heard about the passports, he said not to worry. "Let's wait and see if Mr. Ganert calls us," he said.

By Monday, though, there was still no call from Mr. Ganert. The Aldens' attempts to find out more about the turtle on the Internet had been unsuccessful. Googling *black and orange turtle* brought up images of an interesting type of real turtle, an Eastern box turtle, but no pottery turtles.

They had better luck with the words on the business card. Jessie typed the words into a Latin translation site. "It works!" she exclaimed. "*Ar-te per-en-net* means 'Art endures.'"

"I like that. It means art lasts a long time," Violet explained to Benny.

"What about the other words on the back?" Henry asked.

Jessie typed in *confert Latinum*. She laughed at what came up on the screen. "'Latin helps.' That's not the best way to give us a clue—by telling us in Latin the words are in Latin."

"So we know a little, but we still don't know anything about the turtle," Violet said.

"Maybe it's time to visit the library," Henry suggested. "We can't make any more progress here. And it's a good time for a bike ride. It's not supposed to rain this morning."

They were all happy to get outside. When they reached the library and parked their bikes in the bike rack, Henry pointed at all the other bikes filling the spaces. "It must be busy inside. Look at all the other bikes."

He was right. The library was full of people. The children stood in the entrance. "What do we do first?" Benny asked.

"Let's divide up what we need to do," Jessie suggested.

"I'll try to find out about the turtle," Violet volunteered. "Benny, you can help me since you like it so much."

"Then Jessie and I will try to figure out the Reddimus clue," Henry said. "We'll be sitting over there at that table. Come get us if you figure out something or if you need help." Henry and Jessie found a table and sat down.

Violet told Benny, "The colors on the turtle remind me of the pottery we saw when we were in New Mexico. Why don't we start with books about Native American nations from the Southwest? That will help narrow down our search a little. If I'm wrong, we can move on to other regions."

"Okay, how do we do that?" Benny asked.

"First, we need to look up the right call numbers for the section of art books on Native American pottery," Violet explained. She showed Benny how to use the library computer to look up the information they needed. When she and Benny went to find the books, some were too high on the shelf for them to reach.

"Let's ask a librarian to help us," Benny suggested.

"I only see one librarian, and I don't recognize her," Violet said. "She must be new."

"Which one?" Benny asked. He didn't know the librarians as well as Violet did.

"The woman with her leg in a cast. Look, her cast is purple! And she had a purple streak in her hair! We are seeing lots of purple these days." Violet noticed the new librarian watching them. The woman was putting away a book on a shelf while using one crutch to balance. As soon as the librarian was finished, she headed back to her desk, waving to Benny and Violet as she went by.

"She doesn't look so busy now," Benny said.

Curious about Reddimus Curiosities

When the two went up to her, the librarian smiled at them. "I could tell you needed help. I'm Trudy. What can I do for you?" Her name tag said her name was Trudy Silverton. In front of her on her desk, Violet noticed a pile of markers and a piece of paper with a big question mark on it. The question mark was in all different colors.

Violet leaned in closer. "The question mark is made up of lots of little words all in a line! That's pretty," Violet said.

"It is pretty, isn't it," Trudy said. "It's a form of word art. You pick a shape you want to draw, and then you make the shape by writing little words where you would normally draw the lines." The librarian picked up a blank piece of paper and a marker. "See, if I wanted to make a picture of a bird, I could write 'chirp, chirp, chirp' one after another and curve the words around in the shape of the bird's back and then its head." She wrote a few words and then set the marker down. "It takes a little while to do a whole picture, but it's fun and easy. I'm going to do a session here at the library for people who are interested in learning more about this kind of art."

Curious about Reddimus Curiosities

"I'd like to try that," Violet said. "I like all kinds of arts and crafts. We're here today because we are trying to find out more about a piece of art, a type of pottery, but we can't reach the books we need. Could we use a stool to get them?"

"I'd be glad to help you," Trudy said, getting up from her desk.

"It might be hard for you with your cast." Violet glanced at the cast. It covered most of Trudy's leg.

"Oh, I've gotten good at managing," Trudy said. They followed her to the right shelf and took the books as Trudy handed them down. "You are sure to find what you need," the librarian said as she helped them find a spot to sit down. "These are the right books."

Violet didn't know why Trudy sounded so sure, but she thanked the librarian and then she and Benny got to work.

"How do we start?" Benny asked. "Do I look for a picture of a turtle?"

Violet picked a book and opened it. "You could, but you might not find a turtle. There won't be pictures of every type of Native American pottery."

"So how will we know?" Benny took another book.

"The designs and the orange and black colors on it are important," Violet said. "We learned that different groups used certain colors based on what kind of glazes they could make from the rocks and minerals around them. Now potters can buy the glazes in the colors they want. It's a lot easier, though I think it would be fun to make glazes."

For the next several minutes, they flipped through the pages. Benny liked all the different pictures of animals on different shapes of pottery. He decided he wanted to learn to make pottery too.

He was about to pick up another book when Violet cried, "I found something!" She showed him a picture of some black and white pottery. "I don't know what the I and the K mean, but Acoma is the name of one of the Native American Pueblos in New Mexico."

"What's a pueblo?"

"The book says the word has some different meanings. It means 'town' in Spanish. It's also the word used for some Native American nations and their cultures. There are several Pueblos in the southwestern part of the United States. The Acoma one is in New Mexico."

Benny jumped up from his seat. "Let's go tell Jessie and Henry!"

"Tell us what?" Henry asked as he and Jessie came up to the table. "We have something to tell you, but let's hear you first." Violet explained about Acoma Pueblo.

"Good job, Violet!" Jessie said, a big grin appearing on her face. "Here's what we figured out. I thought Reddimus was someone's last name, but then we realized it doesn't sound like a name we've heard before. Our only other clues were words in Latin, so I had the idea that *reddimus* might be Latin too, and it is! We looked it up in a Latin dictionary. *Reddimus* is a Latin word meaning 'we return.'"

"So we found two important clues!" Benny said.

Jessie's smile faded. "Except we still don't know how to find Mr. Ganert or Reddimus Curiosities."

Henry sighed. "We still haven't solved this mystery."

"Trudy, the new librarian, is staring at us," Violet whispered.

The Secretive
Silverton Family

"We're making too much noise. Let's go home. It's almost time for lunch." Henry and Jessie helped Violet and Benny carry the books to the return cart, and then all the Aldens walked to the door of the library.

As Henry pushed open the door, they heard Trudy's voice. "Wait!" she called as she hobbled toward them. She carried a thin leather-bound book. It looked old.

"You forgot this," Trudy said, handing it to Henry.

"No, this isn't our book," Henry said, trying to hand it back.

Trudy refused to take it back. "It's checked out

in your name. I think you will find it very useful, especially once you open it."

"Miss Silverton!" the other librarian called.

"I'm sure I'll see you soon," Trudy said to the Aldens as she turned to go back to her desk.

"That's odd," Violet said. "Why does she want us to take this book? What's it called? It doesn't have at title on the cover."

"Let's go outside and talk," Henry said.

They took the book over to the bike rack. Henry opened it up, revealing the book had only a few pages in it. The strangest part of it was that all the pages were blank.

"It's not even a real book," Violet said.

"And it's not a library book," Jessie added. "There aren't any numbers or stickers on the spine."

Henry flipped through the pages. "Look at this." He pulled out two pieces of loose paper that had been stuck between two pages. "There is a note and a folded piece of paper. The note says *Bring the turtle. Come to the museum at 8:00 tonight.*" He unfolded the other piece of paper and held it out for the rest of them to see. "It's a map of Greenfield that someone drew."

Jessie took it from him and studied it. "There is a square on it labeled Silverton Mansion."

"Does it show the location of the museum?" Violet asked. "I didn't even know there was a museum in Greenfield."

"It doesn't have anything marked as a museum," Henry said, looking over Jessie's shoulder at the map. "I don't remember ever seeing the Silverton Mansion either."

"I know where it's at," Jessie said. "The mansion is at the edge of town by the old railroad, but it's set back from the road and hidden by a bunch of big trees. I don't know anything about a museum though."

"How are we going to go to a museum tonight if we don't know where it is?" Benny asked.

"We should ask Grandfather." Violet pulled her bike out of the rack. "If there is a museum in Greenfield, he'll know where it's located."

Back at home, the Aldens found Grandfather reading the newspaper in the living room. "I've known the Silverton family for a long time," he said when the children told him about the message and the map. "They once helped the Alden family out, and we've always been grateful to them for it. But that's a long story for another time. The Silverton family made their fortune over a century ago. They built and sold luxury railroad coaches. Much fancier than your boxcar." Grandfather ruffled Benny's hair. "Their coaches had velvet sofas and crystal chandeliers and beautiful woodwork."

"That doesn't sound like our boxcar," Benny said.

"Maybe we could add a chandelier to it!" Violet suggested.

"No," Benny looked horrified. "I don't want a fancy boxcar to play in. I like it just the way it is."

"What about the museum?" Henry asked. "Where is it?"

Grandfather pointed at the house on the map. "It's right here. Most people don't remember it, if they ever knew about it. Once train travel became less popular, the Silvertons opened an unusual private railroad museum behind their mansion. There were some of the old train cars on display. But the museum hasn't been open for many years. The family is reclusive. They keep to themselves."

"Why would they want us to go there tonight?" Jessie asked. "I don't understand any of this."

Grandfather smiled. "It's an unusual way to invite us to their house, but there are many things about the Silvertons that are unusual. You will find the visit very interesting."

The rest of the day passed quickly because Mrs. McGregor had a whole list of errands she needed the children to do for her. After they finished, they ate a quick dinner, and then it was time to go.

"Bring Watch along too. He'll enjoy the car ride,"

Grandfather said as he picked up his keys and went to pull the car out of the garage.

"I'm surprised Grandfather wants Watch along," Jessie said. "We don't usually take him to strangers' houses."

"Grandfather is being thoughtful," Benny told her. "He knows Watch likes car rides."

Jessie wasn't so sure that was the reason. "I'll get the turtle," she said.

Mrs. McGregor came out on the front steps with them and hugged them all. "Have a good time," she said.

"We'll be back in a few hours, Mrs. McGregor," Jessie said, wondering why the housekeeper was seeing them off. The others didn't notice. They were too excited to go to the Silvertons.

The Silverton Mansion was on a narrow road lined with trees. There were no other houses nearby. It was so dark, Grandfather didn't see their driveway at first. He drove right by it and had to turn around. The driveway itself was so overgrown that leaves brushed against the car as Grandfather drove down it.

"I don't see a house," Violet said. "Is this the right place?"

"It's a long driveway," Grandfather replied. "Though I'm surprised I don't see any lights from the house."

The car wound around until the headlights of the car showed a big stone mansion ahead. The lane turned into a big circular driveway in front of the house. They still couldn't see any lights. Large, overgrown bushes nearly blocked the steps up to the house.

"It's creepy," Benny said. "Are you sure someone lives here?"

"As I remember, the museum is in the back of the house. Let's try there," Grandfather said. He backed up the car and took a small paved driveway along the side of the house.

When they came around the side of the house, the children were stunned by what they saw. A small brick rail station sat by train tracks that ran through the backyard. On the tracks in front of the station stood an old-fashioned steam engine. Attached to it were seven train coaches. They were all just as old as the engine, but they looked brand new.

"Wow! Imagine having a whole train in your backyard!" Henry exclaimed.

"It's like we've gone back in time," Jessie said.

Grandfather parked and they all jumped out. "There is no caboose," Benny said. "That train car on the end has too many windows."

"You should ask the Silvertons about that." Grandfather motioned to the second coach back from the engine. I suggest we check out that one since it's the car with all the lights on." As they walked toward the coach, a figure appeared in its doorway. They couldn't tell who it was because of the bright light coming from behind the person.

It made Henry nervous. "Hello!" he called. The figure didn't answer but did hold up a hand as if to greet them.

They drew close enough to tell it was a man. "I think it's Mr. Ganert," Violet whispered.

"Yes it is," Grandfather said. He greeted the man, who just nodded his head and motioned them inside. Inside, it was just as Grandfather had described, with beautiful woodwork and chandeliers and old-fashioned furniture. Violet noticed something that didn't fit. The word-art picture of the question mark that Trudy had made at the library was now hanging on one of the walls in a gold frame.

A familiar voice called out, "Hello, Aldens!" It was Trudy. She sat on a small sofa with her cast propped up on a footstool. "Come in!" They were relieved she sounded so friendly. An elderly woman dressed in dark clothes sat on the edge of one of the large armchairs, her hands crossed in her lap. Her silvery hair was pulled back in a bun. She wasn't smiling. Jessie thought she looked stern.

"Mr. Alden, how nice to see you again," the older woman said to Grandfather. "Please sit down."

Grandfather introduced the children. Mrs. Silverton smiled at them. It made her look a little less severe. "Your grandchildren have already met my grandchild. Mr. Alden, this is my granddaughter Trudy. Welcome to our museum."

"This is a beautiful train car," Jessie said.

"It is delightful, isn't it," Mrs. Silverton agreed. "It is called a parlor car and it was built for a wealthy family who used it to travel between their homes in New York and Florida. We were very pleased to add it to the museum."

No one said anything for a moment. The children were all wondering why they had been asked to come.

Mrs. Silverton looked at each one of them before finally saying, "We've heard many reports of the good work you do in solving mysteries. That's why you are here tonight."

"Do you have a mystery you want us to solve?" Benny asked.

"In a way. You've already solved a mystery we set for you. When the matter of the turtle arose, we decided to see if you could complete some of our tests."

"Tests?" Jessie asked.

"You figured out some information about the turtle and Reddimus Curiosities."

Henry leaned forward. "Did the Reddimus people take the turtle out of the trunk before they loaded it on the truck as part of the test?"

Mrs. Silverton nodded her head. "We did. It was part of the test."

"I don't understand," Jessie said. "What about the man who gave us the flyer? Did he put the turtle in the trunk in the first place?"

Mrs. Silverton shook her head. "That part of this business is very strange. The person who gave you the flyer does not work for us, and we are not sure who he is. He must have been the one to put the turtle in your house, but we don't know why he would do that. When Mr. Alden called us, we were shocked to hear about the incident. That's what set this all in motion."

"We've made some inquiries," Trudy added, "but we haven't been able to learn much. I think if this man knows about us, he may have wanted us to return the turtle to its rightful place."

"So the turtle is yours. Was it stolen from Reddimus Curiosities?" Violet asked.

Mrs. Silverton nodded at Trudy as if she was encouraging Trudy to speak. "No, it doesn't belong to us," Trudy said. "Reddimus Curiosities is an antique store that exists only to be a cover for something much more important, the Reddimus Society. As you figured out, *reddimus* means 'we return.' The Reddimus Society returns things."

Jessie was confused. She glanced over at Henry. He looked as puzzled as she felt. Their confusion must have shown on their faces because Mrs. Silverton said, "Let me explain more about how the Reddimus Society started. The founders, my great-grandparents, were archaeologists."

"Archeologists dig up old things made by people a long time ago, don't they?" Benny asked.

"Archeologists can do that," Mrs. Silverton replied. "Their main job is to try to learn about how people lived in the past. They study a culture's buildings and art and writings, among other things. But you're right, Benny. Sometimes they do dig up sites that have been buried over time from cultures that no longer exist. They also study the histories of people living today. Not every bit of history is written down, so it's useful to add to our knowledge whenever we can. When my great-grandparents started the society, they were upset that some archeologists took ancient artifacts and sold them to collectors. Those archeologists didn't care about the educational value of the items or about the people whose ancestors had created the items."

Mrs. Silverton nodded at Trudy. "Why don't you continue our story," she said to her granddaughter.

"The mission of the Reddimus Society is to return lost treasures to the museums and historic sites where they belong," Trudy explained. "I'm sad to say that even now people take items that don't belong to them to sell or to keep for themselves. But we return these items very quietly. We don't want attention drawn to our work. It would make our tasks more difficult."

Mrs. Silverton touched the broach she wore on her blouse. Violet noticed it matched the Reddimus logo. "That's why we have an owl as part of our symbol. The owl is a very quiet and stealthy creature." Her expression grew more serious. "And that's why it's very troubling someone gave the turtle to you. They obviously know about us, but the Reddimus Society is supposed to be a secret."

CHAPTER 5

A Request for Help

"So are you like secret agents?" Benny asked.

Trudy and Mrs. Silverton laughed. "Not exactly, though we are good at keeping secrets," Mrs. Silverton said. "And now we are in need of more people to help us. We don't have as many agents as we used to. We do have some helpers at different places around the world, but they have other responsibilities as well. For health reasons, I don't travel anymore. Mr. Ganert has his own important job."

"And I can't travel for a while," Trudy added, pointing to her cast. "I'm going to need to have more surgery on my leg. Next time I have to cross a rope bridge in the jungle to find stash of stolen artifacts, I'll make sure the rope isn't rotted."

A Request for Help

"Where did that happen?" Violet asked. "It sounds scary."

"It was more exciting than scary, at least until I fell," Trudy replied.

"But that's a story for another day," Mrs. Silverton said. "After Trudy's accident, we realized this would be a good time to recruit some new members. We need more people we can trust who are good at solving unexpected problems." Mrs. Silverton looked over at Grandfather. "Mr. Alden has always said that we could call on him at any time, so we took him up on the offer, but just to make sure you were up for the tasks we have, we set a few little tests for you."

"What is the task?" Henry asked.

"We've collected several very special items that need to be returned to the countries where they belong," Mrs. Silverton said. Jessie's thoughts raced ahead, thinking of all the postcards on her mobile. *Would the Aldens get to go to some of those places?*

"Of course, we can't send you around the world," Mrs. Silverton continued, "but we'd like you all to return the turtle to Acoma Pueblo. Once you do, we'd also like you to find the Reddimus agent who will deliver the other six items to various spots around the world."

"We'd go all the way to New Mexico?" Violet asked.

"That's the plan," Trudy said. "But you can choose not to go. What we are asking you to do is not exactly a vacation."

Jessie was a little disappointed at first. New Mexico wasn't a different country, but then she remembered it was very different from Connecticut. "Can we, Grandfather?" she asked.

"Yes, we certainly can," Grandfather replied.

"Yay!" Benny and Violet cheered at the same time.

Mrs. Silverman said, "Excellent. We are trusting you with some very special items, so we are counting on you to take good care of them."

"We will," Henry promised.

Mr. Ganert spoke up, surprising the Aldens. They'd almost forgotten he was there. "I'll say it one more time. I think this is a bad idea. These children are too young to be trusted with such important items."

"I've taken your opinion into account, Mr. Ganert," Mrs. Silverton said. "They will have enough help along the way to complete this task. I believe they can do it."

Mr. Ganert got up and walked away from them to stand by the door of the coach. "Very well," he said. "If something goes wrong, it won't be my responsibility."

Trudy glanced at Mr. Ganert and then looked back at the Aldens. She opened a cloth bag on the seat next to her. "I have something for you as our new Reddimus Society helpers. These might come in handy." She pulled out four black flashlights, each small enough to fit in a pocket. Each had a small owl etched in silver on the handle. The etchings looked like the owl in the Reddimus logo. "The special thing about these flashlights is that you can change the color of the lenses if you need to."

Unscrewing a cap on the end of the flashlight, Trudy took out two lenses, a red one and a yellow one. "If your eyes are adjusted to the dark and you want to keep them that way, use the red lenses. It helps preserve your night vision. You can use the yellow one if you are in smoke or fog. It shines through those better than a clear light. The lenses just snap over the top of the flashlight when you need them."

A Request for Help

"Awesome!" Henry said. The children took their lights and experimented with changing the lenses. Benny thought it was one of the best things he'd ever been given. They were so interested in the flashlights, they barely noticed a sound from the front of the train. It sounded as if someone was starting the engine.

"When do we leave?" Jessie asked.

Trudy grabbed her crutches and Mr. Ganert stood up. "Now," Mr. Ganert said. He offered his hand to Mrs. Silverton and helped her out of her chair. They walked to the door. Jessie was confused. How could they be leaving right now? She got up too.

Trudy smiled and motioned for Jessie to sit back down. She took a business card out of her bag and handed it to Henry. "Contact me if you have any trouble. We've arranged all your travel for you," she said as she pushed herself up and out of the chair with her crutches. Mr. Ganert helped Mrs. Silverton down the steps and then tried to help Trudy. "Thank you, I'm fine," Trudy said. As she stepped off the train, she called, "Good luck! Be careful!"

Benny felt a strange sensation beneath his feet. Watch barked. "The floor is rumbling!" he cried. "The train is moving!"

"It can't be!" Violet said, running over to look out the window. She was shocked to see that Benny was right. The train was moving forward, picking up speed.

"Runaway train!" Benny said, excitedly.

"I wouldn't call it *runaway*." Grandfather chuckled. "I think it's *supposed* to be moving."

Jessie turned to Grandfather. She couldn't believe he was just sitting in his chair, laughing and calm.

"We're really going right now, aren't we?" she asked Grandfather.

He nodded his head, looking pleased at the surprise.

Henry leaped up and dashed to the door. "Trudy, wait!" he called "You didn't tell us the name of the person who gets the items."

CHAPTER 6

On the Runaway Train

Trudy waved and then yelled back, "You'll figure it out!"

"It sounds like another test," Jessie said.

"One I'm sure you will pass." Grandfather leaned back in his chair. "We've got a long trip ahead of us, so you'll have plenty of time to think about how to go about finding the person."

"You don't seem surprised we are on a sudden train trip," Henry said to him.

"I'm not. Mrs. Silverton and I discussed all of this over the phone. I'm pleased we can finally do something for them. It should be quite a trip."

Violet moved over to a chair where she could see out the window. The train picked up speed and steam billowed back from the engine. A dark shape caught her eye. At first she thought they had just passed something sitting by the track, but then she saw it was moving at the same speed as the train.

"Someone is running alongside the train!" she cried. The others crowded around the window. The train went even faster. It began to turn as the track curved away from the house.

"I don't see anyone," Henry said.

"Maybe we just went by a tree close to the tracks," Jessie suggested.

"It really was a person," Violet protested. "Trees don't have legs and arms."

Henry moved away from the window. "I don't know why someone would be running by the train. Whoever it was, we've left them behind now."

"We forgot to ask one other important question," Jessie said. "Where are the items we are supposed to deliver? We have the turtle, but nothing else."

Violet looked out the window one more time. There was nothing there. She turned to the others. "Is it another test?"

"That's a lot of tests," Benny said.

Their conversation was interrupted when a young man in a dark purple uniform with silver braid and silver buttons came in through the door at the back of the car. "Good evening," he said. Violet noticed his hat had the Reddimus logo on it. She tried not to stare at his nose, which was very large for the size of his face. His old-fashioned wire-rimmed glasses and his slicked-back hair made him look as if he'd been a part of the train crew back when the cars were brand new.

"I'm your porter for this trip." The man grinned. "Actually, I'm your porter, your chef, and your waiter. I usually do other jobs for the Reddimus Society, but I was needed on this trip, so here I am. Emilio Ortiz at your service. We pride ourselves on taking on any job that needs to be done. The only thing I don't do is get the engine running and the train going in the right direction. That's the job for the driver and the fireman."

"What do you usually do?" Benny asked. "Are you one of their secret agents?"

Emilio winked. "That would be telling."

On the Runaway Train

"Do you know all about the train? Can we see the other cars?" Violet asked.

"Tonight I'll show you the dining car and the Pullman car where you will sleep. It's getting late though, so I'll give you a tour of the other cars tomorrow."

"Why isn't there a boxcar?" Benny asked. "I thought passenger trains always had a few boxcars too."

Emilio stood up very straight and clasped his hands in front of him as if he were going to give a speech. "As more and more people traveled by train, train companies tried new ways of attracting passengers. Some added observation cars on the backs of trains so passengers could sit and enjoy the view. That's what this train has. Boxcars or baggage cars were moved up right behind the engine. We've got a baggage car there. Now I expect all the excitement tonight has made you hungry."

"Yes!" Benny cried.

"I knew it," Emilio said. "Benny, I understand you are quite fond of cookies."

Benny's eyes grew wide. "How did you know that?"

"And how did you know Benny's name?" Jessie asked.

"I know all your names," Emilio replied. "And all your likes and dislikes. I even know what kind of dog food Watch eats, and I've got some on board. We members of the Reddimus Society like knowledge, remember?" He motioned them to follow him. "This way to the dining car. It's the next car behind this one. Watch your step. On these old trains when we go from car to car, we have to go out one door onto a little platform and then into the next coach through another door, so we'll be outside for a few seconds. Don't be surprised at how windy it can feel. Watch won't be scared, will he?" Emilio asked.

"I'll keep a tight hold on his leash," Henry said.

Inside the dining car, they walked down a narrow passageway past a tiny kitchen. "The chefs prepared terrific meals in such small spaces back then. I'm not quite sure how they did it," Emilio said. "I do fine in there by myself cooking for just a few people, but I can't imagine trying to cook for thirty or forty people at a time. And here's the dining room," Emilio moved out of their way so they could see.

"Wow," Violet said. "More chandeliers!"

"It's very fancy," Benny said. "Especially just for milk and cookies." White tablecloths covered each table. On top of them sat vases of flowers and silver salt and pepper shakers.

"Wait until you see it all set up with china and crystal for breakfast," Emilio said. "Train dining cars were like fine restaurants. It was a real treat to eat in one. We have quite a long way to go. If you would like to see our route, I've laid out a map on one of the tables and marked our journey in red, so you can follow along. We'll be going west to Chicago and then heading southwest to Santa Fe."

Benny traced his finger across the country. "New Mexico is a long way from Connecticut."

"Yes, it is. We'll cross several states. It's so far, we are going to make a stop in an hour for another engine. It's going to be attached to the front of the train to pull the steam engine and all our cars.

Old steam engines need too much water and fuel to travel such long distances. Even with a modern engine, it will take us a little more than two days to get there as long as we stay on tracks."

"Why wouldn't we stay on the tracks?" Benny asked.

Emilio made a silly face. Everyone laughed. "It was just a little train humor," he said. "Say, do you want to hear a train joke?"

"Sure," Benny said. "I like jokes."

"Why don't elephants like to ride on trains?" Emilio asked.

"I don't know," Benny said.

The porter grinned. "Because they hate leaving their trunks in the baggage car." He chuckled. "Get it? Trunks?"

Benny laughed. "I get it. That's a good joke."

"Oh, I've got plenty more. They can wait until tomorrow though. Why don't you all have a seat and I'll bring you some milk and cookies? I'll be right back."

The Aldens examined the map while they waited for Emilio. Henry looked at the mileage key on the map and then used his hand to measure the distance. "I estimate it's about two thousand miles following the route that's marked," he said.

Benny yawned. "I'm glad we can sleep some of the way and that someone else is driving the train. I'm getting tired."

Emilio came back in carrying a tray with a pitcher of milk and four glasses. His expression had changed. A frown replaced the smile.

"I was sure I had a box of cookies among the supplies," he said. "I don't see them anywhere. I don't understand how they disappeared. There's no one on the train who would take them."

Violet hadn't thought about how they were the only ones on the train besides the driver and the fireman. It was a little spooky thinking about all the empty cars.

"You'll have to settle for just milk tonight," Emilio added. "I'm sorry."

"That's all right," Jessie assured him. Benny was disappointed but didn't say anything. He knew he could look forward to breakfast.

When they were finished, Emilio said, "Let's

show you where you will sleep. The Pullman sleeper car is the next car back."

They walked through to the sleeper car. It was as fancy as the other cars, though it looked more like a modern train car with pairs of seats facing each other.

"Last time we were on a train, we slept in little compartments," Violet said. "I don't see any, unless that part at the back has compartments."

"It does, but there are only two in this car. I thought your grandfather would like one."

"I would," Grandfather said. "That way I can snore as much as I want."

"So do we all sleep in the other one?" Benny asked.

"No, I'll show you where you sleep in a few minutes," Emilio replied. "But I forgot, I have some things for you in the next car back. You will get to see another car tonight after all. Why don't you come with me to help carry your things back in here?"

"Great!" Benny said. "I can't wait to see the whole train."

On the Runaway Train

Emilio motioned for the Aldens to follow him. "Be careful," he said as he led them down to the end of the dining car. "Several of the lights in the other car aren't working for some reason. They were fine earlier this evening, but when I came through there a little while ago, some were out and others were flickering. We'll have to get them checked out. The wiring in that car is the original. We've added some modern conveniences like Wi-Fi and air conditioning, but we haven't updated everything."

There was a light on over the door of the car, but once inside only a few other lights were on. It was difficult to see much besides some dark furniture shapes. "This is a library car," Emilio explained. "When this train was in use for passengers, it had all the latest newspapers and magazines, along with books. There's even a writing desk for passengers who wanted to write letters or postcards. Tomorrow you'll be able to see it better in the daylight if we can't get the lights fixed."

He walked over to a table against one side of the train and pulled something out from under it.

"It's our trunk!" Jessie cried.

Benny ran over and put his hands on top of it. "I thought we wouldn't see it again."

Violet joined him. "I didn't either. I've been thinking I would miss seeing it in the study."

"We needed to bring it along," Emilio said. "You'll see why."

The Aldens were surprised to see the trunk had a new combination lock on it. They'd never locked it before. Emilio turned the dial of the lock until it opened, then he lifted the lid of the trunk.

Henry looked inside. "It's got our backpacks in it." He took them out of the trunk and handed them to his brother and sisters.

"My laptop is in there too!" Jessie cried. She liked to keep it with her to look up information if they couldn't get to a library.

"There's one more bag." Violet reached in and took out a small dark-brown leather suitcase.

"I believe that one is mine," Grandfather said.

"Who packed our things?" Jessie asked.

Grandfather's eyes twinkled. "Mrs. McGregor did. I let her in on the plan."

Jessie understood why Mrs. McGregor had

hugged them. She knew they were going on a trip.

Benny leaned over and peered in the trunk. "There's something else in there."

On the bottom of the trunk were six little boxes wrapped in newspaper and tied with twine.

Emilio picked one up. "These are the items you will deliver to the Reddimus agent. I've got a bag for you to put them in. I'll give it to you tomorrow."

"I'm glad they are here, so we don't have to figure out where they are. That's one less test we have to pass," Benny said.

Violet frowned. "They don't look very special just wrapped in old newspaper."

"They aren't supposed to look special," Emilio explained. "You might say they are disguised. Inside each wrapped parcel is a locked wooden box that doesn't look very special either. And inside that is a very special box, also locked. It's very sturdy and padded on the inside. Museums use those sorts of boxes to transport small valuable items so they don't get damaged." Emilio noticed Benny yawning.

"We can talk about the boxes more tomorrow,"

the porter said. He put the box back in the trunk and locked it. "Since you are going to be in charge of the items, I'll give you the combination. It's 1859. Can you remember that?" The Aldens all nodded, even though Benny wasn't sure he really could remember.

"Now, let me show you your beds. You go first. I want to shut off the lights." Back in the Pullman car, the porter showed the Aldens how the lower seats could be changed into beds by sliding them together. "Each bed can be separated by curtains," he said, taking off the ties that were holding the curtains against the wall and pulling them toward him.

"And if you like to sleep up high, you can have an upper berth." He unhooked a clasp on a panel near the ceiling, lowering the panel down to reveal a mattress, blankets, and pillows.

"Everything for both the upper and lower berth is stored here," Emilio explained as he took down what he needed. They helped him make up the beds.

When everyone had enough pillows and

blankets, Emilio said, "Who wants to sleep in the upper berths?"

"I do!" Violet and Benny said at the same time.

"That's good," Jessie said, "Because I'd like a lower berth. Those have windows and are a little bigger."

"Yes, I'd like a lower berth too," Henry said.

"Excellent! I'm glad everyone can be where they want to be," Emilio said.

"How do we get up there?" Benny asked.

"I'll be right back." Emilio went to a small storage compartment at the back of the car and pulled out two wooden ladders, attaching each one to the edge of an upper berth. "And if you want, you can close the curtains around the beds."

"How do we do that?" Benny asked.

"I just noticed the brass rods," Henry said, pointing up to the ceiling. "That's how you close them." Emilio showed them how to unfasten the curtains and draw them across the rods.

"That's everything," Emilio said. "I'll see you in the morning. I'll be in my berth, which is in the baggage car right behind the engine. Good night."

Once everyone had their pajamas on and were ready for bed, Grandfather went to his compartment. The children climbed into their berths and turned off their lights. Watch lay down in the aisle.

Even though Benny had been sleepy before, he found he was still too excited to go to sleep. For a while, he listened to the *clackety-clack* of the train going over the rails and the chugging of the engine. He decided he'd turn on the light above his bed and then climb down to get a book out of his backpack. But the light didn't work. He remembered his new flashlight. Where was it?

He pulled open the curtains and leaned over the edge of his berth. "Henry, Jessie," he whispered. "Are you awake?"

There was no answer from either of them, but Violet opened up her curtains and said, "What's wrong, Benny?"

"I don't know what I did with my flashlight."

Violet raised herself up on one arm and looked over at Benny. "It's probably in the pocket of your jeans. That's where I put mine. So it's probably in your backpack with your jeans. Why don't you look?"

Benny turned his light back on and climbed down the ladder, trying to be quiet so he wouldn't wake up Henry and Jessie. He rummaged around in his backpack, which was on the seat nearest to their berths. "It's not here. Maybe I dropped it in the parlor car when the train started to move. No, wait. I remember. I did put it in my pocket, because I started to take it out in the library car when Emilio said some of the lights were out."

"You probably dropped it in there then. We can find it in the morning." Violet gave a loud yawn. "Good night."

Benny climbed back up into his berth and tried to go to sleep, but he couldn't stop thinking about the flashlight. He could go look, he told himself. No one said he had to stay in his bed. It would be awful if he could not find the flashlight. Mrs. Silverman wouldn't like it if he lost the first thing they'd been given. That would be failing a test for sure.

He climbed back down the ladder. In the dim light, the train car seemed bigger and longer than he remembered. Watch got up and wagged his tail. "You'll go with me, right, Watch?" Benny said. Remembering he and Watch would have to go outside the Pullman car to get to the door to the library car, he put the dog's leash back on him.

"We'll only be outside for a few seconds, Watch, right? You won't mind that." Taking a firm hold of Watch's leash, Benny walked down the aisle toward the door. When he opened it, he was glad to see the library car was still lit, though with so many of the lights out, it still wasn't all that bright. He took a step toward it and then remembered Emilio had said he was going to turn off all the lights in the car. Had he? Benny couldn't remember.

"Benny!" A voice came from behind him. "What are you doing?" It was Violet.

"I really want to find my flashlight," he said. "I'm going to go look for it."

"You shouldn't go by yourself," his sister told him. "If I go with you, will you come back to bed even if we don't find it?"

"Yes," Benny said, glad Violet had volunteered to come too.

On the Runaway Train

When they went into the library car, Benny stopped so fast that Violet ran into him. She started to ask him why he had stopped, when he raised his arm and pointed. There was another person in the car. A woman with a blond ponytail wearing a porter's uniform knelt in front of the trunk. Her back was to them, but they could see she was speaking into a cell phone.

The woman shifted. Light reflected off the woman's shoes. Violet looked more closely and saw the porter wore fancy sneakers with a reflective stripe on each side. They didn't go with the old-fashioned uniform.

"The trunk is locked," the woman said into the phone. "I've got an idea about that problem." As she moved to stand up, Watch growled. The woman leaped up and whirled around, dropping her phone at the sight of them. She was very tall, taller than Grandfather even, and she towered over them. Watch growled again, louder this time.

"What are you doing in here?" the woman demanded.

A Close Call

"I...I lost my flashlight," Benny stuttered.

The woman stared at them for a moment and then reached down and picked up her phone. Her cheeks had bright red blotches on them. She looked angry. "I'll call you back," she said, shutting it off. "I haven't seen a flashlight," she told Benny and Violet. "You should be in bed."

"We came to look for it," Benny said, hoping the woman would offer to help them.

She didn't. Her phone rang. The woman answered it and said, "Hold on a minute." Ignoring Benny and Violet, she walked away from them and went out the door at the back of the car.

"I didn't know there was another porter on

the train," Violet said.

"Maybe Emilio forgot to tell us." Benny looked over at the trunk. "Why was she trying to get in there? She said she had a plan to get them. She meant the boxes, but Emilio said they were our responsibility now."

"I don't know. I don't like this. We should wake someone up and tell them."

"That means we'd have to leave the boxes in the trunk. What if she comes back and takes them?"

"I can go wake up Henry and Jessie and Grandfather and you and Watch can stay and guard the trunk," Violet suggested.

"I don't want to stay here by myself!" Benny cried. "Not even with Watch. I'll go wake people up and you can stay."

"I don't want to stay by myself either." Violet went over to the trunk. "We could take the boxes back with us. That way we know they'll be safe."

"That's a good idea. I've forgotten the combination. It's the man's birthday who wrote the Sherlock Holmes stories, but I didn't remember the year."

"I do," Violet said. "It's 1859."

A Close Call

They opened the trunk and took out the boxes. Violet wrinkled her nose when she pulled out the last box. "I didn't know this trunk was so dirty inside. It's got blotches all over the bottom. It looks like when Grandfather spills his coffee. Maybe he spilled some when he was putting something in the trunk sometime."

Benny leaned over into the trunk so he could see better. "There are a lot of blotches. Whoever it was spilled a lot of coffee. I wish I had my flashlight."

"Here, take mine." Violet handed hers to Benny. He shone it in the bottom of the trunk. "Someone scribbled all over the bottom too." He laughed. "Not Grandfather. He doesn't scribble."

"He might have when he was a baby." They both giggled at that. It was hard to imagine Grandfather as a baby.

The train's whistle sounded, startling them. They jumped up, remembering that the woman could come back in at any time. "Let's go!" Benny said, putting the end of Watch's leash around his wrist and grabbing some of the boxes.

"Let me lock the trunk back up first," Violet said.

"We don't want the lock to get lost in case we need to put the boxes back in it." She closed the lid of the trunk and locked it then picked up the remaining boxes. They hurried back to the sleeper car.

When they got to their section of the car, they felt the train slow down. Henry and Jessie were still sleeping soundly. Benny and Violet set the boxes down on the seat next to the berths. Benny was still worried about them so he put his and Violet's backpacks in front of them to hide them a little more. "Wake up," Benny said. He reached into Henry's berth and shook his brother's shoulder. "Wake up, Henry."

The train slowed even more and then stopped. Jessie woke up. "What's wrong? Why did we stop?"

Henry turned over, opened his eyes, and then sat up when he realized everyone else was awake. "We're stopped," he said as he rubbed his eyes.

"I don't know why we stopped. That's not why we woke you up." Violet explained what happened. She finished by saying, "There was something strange about that porter."

Before anyone could respond, they heard

A Close Call

another train roar by them, so close everything rattled inside the car. Henry got up and looked out the windows on both sides of the train. "We're on a side track," he said. "I suppose we had to move out of the way so the faster train could go by."

"What about that porter? She wasn't very nice," Benny added. "Should we tell Grandfather?"

"No." Henry came back to them. "We don't need to wake up Grandfather. I'm sure it's just a misunderstanding. Why would a Reddimus porter take the boxes?"

"From the way she was talking on the phone, she was planning on taking the boxes," Violet said.

Jessie got up too. "Let's go find her and talk to her. I'm sure she'll explain."

The train began to move again as they went into the library car. The woman wasn't there, and the lock was still on the trunk. "The only other place she could be is in the observation car," Jessie said. "It's the last car on the train. We know she didn't come through the sleeping car because we would have seen her."

Henry yawned. "Yes, let's go. I want to go back to sleep."

The children went into the observation car. It was full of big comfortable chairs next to large windows that lined the sides and back of the car. The four of them walked through the car looking in each chair. All the chairs were empty. At the back of the car, they could see a small viewing platform with a railing on the other side of the door. It was empty too.

"Where could she have gone?" Violet asked.

"Are you sure you really saw someone?" Henry asked.

"Yes! We saw her and we talked to her," Violet insisted.

"Maybe she got off the train when it stopped." Benny went over to a window and looked out. The others joined him, but there was nothing to see but farmland and a few faint lights in the distance.

"I suppose that's the only explanation that makes sense," Henry said. He didn't sound very sure.

Jessie shivered. "I don't like it in here. Let's go back to our own car." Everyone agreed. They were all ready to leave the big empty car.

A Close Call

Back in their berths, Benny said, "Are you sure we shouldn't wake up Grandfather?"

"Yes. We can't do anything else tonight," Henry said. "The boxes are safe with us."

It took them all a long time to fall asleep. Violet woke up first. The train had stopped again. Early morning light came through the windows. She climbed down, intending to get dressed. There was something wrong, but it took her a moment to figure out what it was. Watch was gone. She ran down the aisle, hoping the dog was with Grandfather. The compartment door was open, but neither Grandfather nor the dog was there.

Just as she woke the others, Grandfather and Watch came in.

"I took Watch out for a walk while they are doing a crew change," Grandfather said. "You were all sleeping so soundly I didn't want to wake you."

Emilio came through from the direction of the dining car.

"Good morning! Breakfast is waiting." He stared at their faces "None of you look like you got a good night's sleep."

Henry told Emilio and Grandfather about how Violet and Benny saw the mystery porter trying to get into the trunk. "And when we looked for her, we couldn't find her. We think she got off the train when it pulled over on a side rail."

"Who was she?" Violet asked.

"That wasn't a Reddimus Society member," Emilio said, a panicked look appearing on his face. "I need to check the trunk." He hurried toward the library car. The Aldens followed.

When they reached the next car, they were shocked to see an empty space where the trunk had been sitting. "She took the trunk!" Emilio said. "I have to tell the engineer to stop the train so we can go back!" He rushed toward the door.

"Young man!" Grandfather called, hurrying after him. "I don't think that's the best idea."

Emilio kept going. Grandfather followed.

Benny had a horrible thought. "Do you think she found the boxes and took those too while we were sleeping?" he asked.

"I hope not!" Violet raced back to the sleeping car, the rest of the children close behind.

A Close Call

When they reached their berths, they were relieved to see the boxes were still on the seat behind Benny's backpack.

"Whew," Henry said. "Good thing you hid them, Benny."

"Yes, but the trunk is still gone," Jessie said. "What if it was important?"

CHAPTER 8

Something Out of Time

Something else was bothering Henry. "I don't understand how the woman could have taken the trunk. The train stopped and then started again before we came to look for her. She wasn't here, but the trunk still was."

Violet jumped up. "She might have hidden it somewhere else on the train so at the next stop someone else could get it off. Or she might have dragged it out onto the observation platform in the back."

"We looked out there," Benny reminded Violet.

"I'm going to look again," Jessie said. They all followed Jessie to the back of the train. When they got there, they could see that the platform was empty.

Something Out of Time

"What's all over the floor of it?" Benny asked. "Those little bits of things."

They went out. Violet bent down and picked one up. "It's a crumb from a cookie or a muffin or something."

Jessie picked one up too. "Cookie crumb from a sugar cookie. So that's where the missing cookies went. She sneaked into the kitchen last evening and took them. She must have been out here waiting for a chance to get at the trunk. It still doesn't explain where it is now."

"I have an idea," Henry said. He leaned over the railing and looked around the edge of the car. "Train cars usually have a way to get to the roof of each car, like footholds attached to a side or the back. I see some on this one."

Jessie shuddered. "I wouldn't want to climb up it when the train was moving."

"Maybe she climbed up there when we were stopped and is hiding," Henry said.

Violet leaned over to look at the footholds. "I don't know how she'd get the trunk on the roof. It's heavy even when it's empty."

Benny took hold of Jessie's hand. "That's creepy. I don't like the idea of someone sneaking around the train."

"I know, Benny," Jessie said. Something on the road next to the track caught her eye. The train passed a pickup truck traveling down the road. A woman with a blond ponytail looked out the passenger window at the train.

"There she is again!" Violet cried. "And she's got our trunk!" The trunk was sitting in the back of pickup. The pickup slowed down and then turned off on a side road. It headed away from the track and went out of sight as the train left it behind. Emilio and Grandfather came through the door and crowded onto the platform with them.

Henry explained what they thought had happened, adding, "She must have arranged to have someone pick her up at the crew-switch stop," Henry said.

Emilio smacked his hand against his forehead "You're right. And now she's got the boxes. This is bad."

"She doesn't have the boxes. We have the boxes."

Something Out of Time

Benny told him what he and Violet had done the night before.

"Good thinking, you two," Grandfather said.

"That's a relief!" Emilio pulled out a handkerchief, took off his cap and wiped his forehead. Jessie noticed something strange about his face. His nose looked crooked all of a sudden. She didn't remember it being crooked before, and since it was such a big nose, she was sure she would have noticed.

"I don't know how she got on the train in the first place," Emilio said. "I went all through it making sure it was ready for the trip while you were talking to the Silvertons."

"I know," Violet said. "I thought I saw someone running along side the train when it started. I think she jumped on board at the last minute."

"I need to report this." Emilio took out his cell phone and punched in a number. "Mrs. Silverton," he said as he walked back into the observation car. They went inside too, but Emilio kept walking, out of the observation car and into the library car. They heard him say something that sounded like "urgent" as the door shut behind him.

In a few minutes, Emilio came back. "Everything is fine," he said.

"But we heard you say the word 'urgent,'" Violet said. "That doesn't sound like everything is fine."

Emilio frowned. "I didn't say 'urgent.' You just misheard me. Now I have some things I need to do. Breakfast is all laid out in the dining car." He practically ran out of the car.

The Aldens followed more slowly. When they reached the dining car, Emilio wasn't there. He wasn't in the kitchen either.

"I expect he's getting everything sorted out," Grandfather said, helping himself to a pastry. Violet wasn't so sure. She knew she had heard the word "urgent."

When they finished breakfast, Grandfather went to the library car to do some work. The rest of them went back to the Pullman car and got dressed. They folded up their beds and then sat down.

"I don't like not knowing what's happening," Henry said. "And even though we have the boxes, we still don't know who we are delivering them to. How are we supposed to figure that out?"

Something Out of Time

"Trudy told us we could contact her if we needed to," Jessie reminded him. "You've got her card."

Henry got it out of his backpack. "It has her Skype name on it. Emilio said the train has Wi-Fi, so we can call her."

Jessie started up her laptop. Trudy answered immediately, as if she had been expecting them to call. They explained what happened.

"Yes, I heard about it. I didn't want to worry you before," she said, "but there is something you need to know now. The Reddimus Society has, well, an enemy of sorts. There's a greedy family of collectors who run an auction house called Argent Auctions. They want the treasures in the boxes so they can be sold to the highest bidders. I never expected them to send someone to get on our train. From the description, it sounds like it was a woman named Anna Argent. I don't think Anna will try again though. Even once she figures out the trunk is empty, it would be difficult for her to get back on the train and search it."

"That's a relief," Jessie said. She sat back in her chair.

"Trudy, we have another problem," Henry said. "Who gets the items once we get to New Mexico?"

"I was planning on calling you today to give you the hint. There is something on the train that will help you. Look for something that is out of time." She smiled. "I expect Violet will be the one to find it. I have to go now. Bye." She hung up.

They all looked at Violet. She shook her head. "I don't know why I'm supposed to be the one."

"Well, we've got a whole day and night on the train before we arrive," Henry said. "Let's explore. Maybe we will figure something out."

"It could be something like an hourglass," Jessie suggested. "When the sand runs out of an hourglass, it's sort of like it's out of time."

"Good idea!" Violet said. They went all over the train, having fun examining all the antique objects. They didn't find an hourglass or anything else that seemed as if it fit the clue. They asked Emilio if he had any idea what the clue meant, but he said he didn't. He was busy working on his own laptop, and when they came up to him, he closed the lid so they couldn't see the screen.

Something Out of Time

When the children had looked everywhere, they settled back into the parlor car, dejected that they hadn't figured out the clue.

"I don't know what to do next," Henry said.

"Out of time. Out of time," Violet murmured. She was sitting opposite the picture she had noticed the first night, Trudy's word art. It struck her again that it looked odd amongst all the old furniture and decorations.

She jumped up. "I see something that's out of time, at least out of the time of everything else on the train. This is the word-art picture Trudy was working on at the library. It's too modern for the train."

"You're right!" Jessie jumped up too. "Back when these cars were built and decorated, there weren't any markers. Artists would have used paint or colored pencils."

"Yes, and I don't think anyone made this kind of word art," Violet added.

Henry took it off the wall. "What do the words say?" Benny asked.

Henry read it aloud. "History is learned in many ways. Sometimes through stories and sometimes without words. The story on the back will help you find her last name. Look for her in the city in the sky, speaking of lost things."

"It sounds like we need to find a city in the clouds," Benny said. He frowned. "There isn't such a thing, is there?"

"No," Jessie said.

"Let's google 'city in the sky' and see what comes up," Violet suggested.

When they did, thousands of images came up, including pictures of imaginary places and real places with that nickname, but they couldn't find anything in New Mexico.

Even though there were books and games aboard, the Aldens were anxious for the journey to end, so when Emilio told them, "We are about to pull into Albuquerque Station," everyone cheered.

He handed them a small padded duffle bag. It was dark blue and had a strap as well as a handle on it. "This is the bag for all the items." Jessie placed the turtle and all the boxes inside and zipped it up. "Your rental car is waiting for you," he continued. "You can leave Watch and your luggage with me.

I'll deliver them to the Albuquerque airport so after you find the Reddimus agent and return the turtle, you can head straight to the airport to go home." He sounded so sure they would complete the task, they felt more confident about what lay ahead of them.

"Watch, you be good," Benny said as he knelt down to give Watch a hug. The other children said their good-byes too.

"Don't worry. I'll take good care of him," Emilio assured them.

They were about to get off the train when Benny said, "Wait, I can't find my flashlight."

"Look in your backpack," Jessie told him. Benny did, but it wasn't there.

"When did you last have it?" Henry asked.

"He was using it yesterday while we were exploring the train," Violet said. "It could be anywhere."

"You'll have to search for it," Grandfather said. "I need to make a phone call, so I'll go get the rental car and then make my call. You can meet me in front of the train station when you find the flashlight."

The children searched the whole train. Violet finally found the flashlight on a shelf in the library car. "Oh, I remember," Benny said. "I set it down because my shoe came unfastened and I needed to fix it."

"At least it's found now," Jessie said. "Put it in your pocket so it doesn't get lost again. Let's go say goodbye to Emilio and then find Grandfather."

Emilio was cleaning up the kitchen. "All ready to go?" he asked.

They nodded. "I'm sure I'll see you again soon," he said. "Watch and I will walk out with you." As they went through the dining car, Benny looked out the window. He was startled by what he saw. "There is a whole crowd of people out there staring at the train."

"The train is one of the highlights of the railroad festival," Emilio said. "People are excited they are going to get to tour it."

Violet looked out at the crowd too. Behind the crowd, she noticed a white truck parked at an odd angle. The name ARGENT AUCTIONS was painted on the side. It had a logo on it too. The logo looked a little like the Reddimus one, except instead of an R inside a fancy circle, this one had a big silver A inside a plain circle. A tall woman got out of the cab of the truck. She had a blond ponytail. "It's her!" Violet cried. "Anna Argent. The woman who was on the train!"

The woman strode through the crowd toward the train, shoving people aside.

"She's looking right at us!" Benny said.

"This isn't good." Emilio pulled Violet and Benny away from the window. "You need to get out of here. Go through to the parlor car and get off there on the other side. I'll try to distract her."

The Aldens ran through the dining car and into the parlor car, dodging the sofas and chairs. When they reached the far end, they pushed open the door and went out onto the platform. Jessie peeked around the corner of the car. "I don't see her anymore. She might already be on the train!"

"This way!" Henry said. They jumped down, not sure where to go. The station was behind them and there was a commuter train between them and the sidewalk to get to it.

"There," Jessie pointed. "The tracks end up ahead. We can go around the engine to get to the other side." They dashed around the engine and past the commuter train. Many of its cars were double-deckers, which blocked the view of the Silverton train.

Something Out of Time

"She won't be able to see us with that train in the way. Hurry!" Henry said. They ran partway down the platform, but instead of going inside the station they went around the building. They found Grandfather sitting in a rental car, waiting for them.

They piled in the car and Jessie said, "We need to leave right now. Anna Argent is looking for us." As they pulled away from the station, Violet looked out the window in time to see Anna run out the door and stop, looking in all directions. Jessie yelled, "Duck down! We don't want her to spot us!"

But Grandfather was calm. "I think we are far enough away that she couldn't see us," Grandfather said. "She doesn't know what the rental car looks like and she doesn't know where we are going. Everything will be fine. It's not like the items belong to her anyway. She can't just come up to you and demand you give them to her. Mrs. Silverton told me she wouldn't be a problem. I believe her."

Henry hoped Grandfather was right. Neither Grandfather nor Mrs. Silverton had seen the angry look on Anna's face.

For the next two hours, they drove through

a beautiful landscape of mountains and rock formations in all sorts of colors. Some of them even looked gold when the sun hit them at certain angles. When they came to a valley, Benny looked out the window in front of them. "It's a square mountain," he said. "It looks like a giant box made out of rock."

"That's called a mesa," Henry told him. "If you look more closely, you can see buildings on top of it. That's Acoma Pueblo."

"How do we get up there?" Violet asked.

"There are tours," Grandfather said, "But we have to buy our tickets at the area below the mesa. He parked the car by a building with a sign next to it that read Sky City Cultural Center & Haak'u Museum.

Jessie laughed. "We were googling the wrong order of words. It's not a city in the sky, it's Sky City. This is the place in the clue."

"So maybe the Reddimus agent works in the museum!" Violet said, excited by the discovery. "That would make sense. Let's go!"

CHAPTER 9

The City in the Sky

Inside, a young woman sat at a desk issuing tickets for the museum. "We can ask her if she's part of the Reddimus Society," Benny suggested.

"I don't think we should be so obvious," Henry said. "The person we need to find is supposed to speak of lost things. I have an idea." He went up to the woman. "Hello, do you have a lost and found?"

"What did you lose?" the woman asked. "Found items are in a bin in the director's office. I can call and find out if your item is there."

"Oh." Henry said, suddenly at a loss for words. He hadn't expected the woman to ask him about a specific item.

"I didn't lose anything," he told her. "I was just

wondering. Thank you."

The woman gave a confused look and then shrugged, turning to help the next person in line.

They walked away so she couldn't overhear them. "We can't just walk around asking museum employees if they know about lost things," Henry said.

"Let's look around," Jessie said. "I'm sure we will find a clue here." As they explored the museum, the Aldens were amazed to see all the beautiful pottery on display. Some of it had geometric designs in elaborate patterns. Others had images of animals.

"I like the animal ones," Benny said, "But I also like the little pottery people."

"What little pottery people?" Jessie asked, coming over to Benny. Inside the case in front of Benny were pottery figures of people with lots of tiny children sitting on laps and heads and shoulders.

Violet looked at the plaque next to the case. "The description says these are storyteller figures. See how the biggest figures have their mouths open like they are singing or talking? It says the storyteller figurines were first developed by an artist in

another pueblo, the Cochiti Pueblo, to honor the artist's grandfather. He was a storyteller who told about the history of their nation. Some Acoma potters started making storyteller figures too."

"Oh, I like this one too," Benny said. "Look, the children who are listening are sitting on a turtle..." His voice trailed off.

"A turtle," Henry said, leaning over the case to get a better view.

"It's got the same black and orange lines in the same pattern as our turtle!" Violet said. "But we already knew it came from Acoma. That doesn't help much."

Henry pointed at the plaque underneath a photograph of an elderly woman at work on a large clay pot. "Look at the name of the artist. Isabel Keene."

"That's a nice name," Jessie said.

"It is a nice name, but I meant look at the capital letters, *I* and *K*. Just like the *I* and *K* on the bottom of the turtle. *I K A C O M A*. I think it stands for Isabel Keene, Acoma. She made the turtle. We need to find her and give it back to her."

Violet read the information on the plaque

aloud. "Isabel Keene has won many awards for her distinctive pottery. She began to make pots as a child and has continued to experiment with forms and patterns. She uses both traditional designs and those that she developed on her own."

"I don't know if she still lives there, but we can ask if anyone knows her," Jessie said.

They asked the girl at the ticket counter. "She is up on the mesa on some days. I don't know if she is there today," the girl said.

"I've already got tickets for us," Grandfather said. "Let's find our bus."

They boarded the small bus and sat down with the other tourists. Right before the bus pulled away from the parking lot, a young man got on and stood at the front. He talked as the bus headed for the mesa. "Hello, my name is Brian and I am a member of the Acoma Pueblo," he said. "I've lived in this area my whole life. Part of the year, I'm a student at the University of New Mexico. The other part of the year I come home and give tours. I'm studying history at school and plan to become a teacher, so I hope you will have lots of questions for me."

"Do you live on top of the mesa?" a woman asked.

"No. There is no regular supply of electricity and no running water. A few people live at the pueblo full time but most families live in other towns close by. They come up to the mesa to stay for holidays and special ceremonies."

"Why isn't there electricity?" a boy sitting in the front of the bus asked.

"Good question," Brian said. "The Acoma Pueblo is a special place to us. We keep it the way it was in the past to remember and preserve the original Pueblo culture. We want to keep a sense of our history. The pueblo had been occupied for nearly a thousand years, and our people went through many hardships to hold onto the mesa when other peoples tried to conquer the land. Much of the land below the mesa was taken away from us, so we are determined to protect Sky City."

They pulled into a small parking area at the top of the mesa. Before they got out, Brian said, "You will see many pieces of pottery being sold by local potters. We have a very long tradition of making pottery. Many times, the method and steps an artist uses to make the pottery is part of a culture too. So once an object is completed, it can hold a story of its own, both of the artist and of the culture."

One of our most famous potters, Isabel Keene, used to search for pottery shards, which are broken bits of pottery, so that she could learn what designs our potters used hundreds of years ago. She took those designs and then used them to create her own, but in doing so, gave them a special link to the past."

Benny whispered to the other Aldens, "He said the name, Isabel Keene, and he talked about stories. Do you think he is the one?"

"No, remember Benny, we are looking for a girl. The clue said *The story on the back will help you find her last name.*"

"Oh, right, I forgot."

As soon as they got out of the bus, they were surprised at how cool the air felt and how strong the wind was blowing. Bits of sand swirled around their legs.

"It's because we are so high up," Brian explained.

Benny turned slowly around in a circle, as he

looked up at the sky. "The sky is very big here!" he declared.

The tour guide laughed. "It does look big with so much open space around us."

"What a terrific view," Jessie said. Everyone agreed.

They followed Brian around as he told them the history of the pueblo. There were many artists sitting at tables displaying their work. The Aldens walked up to one man.

"Hello," the man said. "Are you enjoying the tour?"

"Very much," Violet replied. She picked up a small pot. "These are terrific. They remind me of the designs Isabel Keene did. We saw a display at the museum about her."

The man nodded. "She is a great artist, and has influenced many of the potters here."

"Do any members of her family live here now?" Jessie asked. "We have something that might belong to her."

Just then the screen door to one of houses opened and a young woman walked out. The first thing the Aldens noticed about her was her purple sweater. The second thing was the silver owl necklace she wore. The children looked at each other. They were all thinking she might be the person they were supposed to find. She brushed her black shiny hair away from her face and they saw her earrings. The earrings had the same black and white pattern that was on some of Isabel Keene's pottery.

"Hello," the woman said. "I could hear you from inside. My name is Christina Keene. I'm Isabel's grand-niece."

"We have something that might belong to Isabel." Jessie took the turtle out of the bag, unwrapped it, and handed it to Christina.

A big smile appeared on Christina's face. "I recognize this. It was stolen from an exhibit of Isabel's work that was on display at a museum in Santa Fe. I swore that if we ever got it back I would help return other lost things," she said. "There are people who do that, you know. It's an important job."

The children exchanged a look: This must be the agent they were looking for! "Speaking of lost things," Henry said. "Have you ever heard of the Reddimus Society?"

Christina winked and then took a cellphone out of her pocket. She punched in a number and then spoke into the phone. "This is Christina Keene, and I'm reporting for duty, Mrs. Silverton." She listened and then said, "I understand. I'll call again before I board the plane."

"So this belongs to you." Jessie handed her the duffle bag that contained all the boxes.

Christina took it and put the strap over her head so the bag rested on her hip. "I'll take good care of it," she said.

Brian walked over to them. "Hi, Christina. It's time our group moved along," he said to the Aldens.

"Hi, Brian," Christina put her phone away. "I'll take charge of this family and have them back to the bus on time," she told him. "They are friends of a friend, and I'd like to talk to them."

Brian hesitated and then said, "Okay, I suppose. Don't lose them. I'm responsible, you know."

"I know. Don't worry. I used to give these tours when I was younger. I never lost anyone."

"All right. See you in a bit. This way," he said, leading the group away.

"If you don't want to take the bus back, I can take you down the original steps cut into the cliff," Christina said to the Aldens. "It's quite an experience, but I have to warn you, the steps are very, very steep. Sometimes you have to use handholds cut into the walls."

Grandfather shook his head. "Not a good way down for me, but it would be fun for the children."

"Yes! Let's do it," Henry said. The others agreed.

"Wonderful." Christina turned to Grandfather. "Mr. Alden, did you get the message from Emilio?"

"I did," he said. "We'd be happy to give you a ride."

"Are you coming with us back to Connecticut before you leave?" Violet asked.

"No. I thought I wasn't leaving for a few days, but the departure has been moved up. The Reddimus plane is waiting for me at a private airfield near the airport. You're going to drop me off there and pick up your dog. Emilio told me Watch is fine. He's made friends with the airfield manager."

"I'm sure he did," Grandfather said. "You'd better

start down so we can get to Albuquerque in time. I'll see you in a little while."

After Grandfather went to rejoin the group, Christina led the Aldens to the top of the path. "We'll go single file," she said. "I'll go first. Just take your time and you won't have any trouble."

Jessie wasn't so sure. She looked down the stone steps that had been notched into the cliff. There were handholds carved into the stones on either side of the path. "Benny, you'll have to be very careful," Jessie warned.

"I will," Benny said.

They started down. Jessie went last, so she could call out to Benny if she thought he was going too fast.

The steps turned out to be easier to get down than they looked, and soon Jessie was happy they'd decided to take the path. She was listening to Violet describe the colors of the stone when a sound came from behind them, and then a woman's voice cried, "Ouch!"

Jessie looked back but the path had curved and she couldn't see anyone. "Are you hurt?" she called, thinking someone might have fallen.

No one answered. Jessie and Violet stopped. They listened but didn't hear any sound.

"That's strange," Jessie said. "Should we go back and look?"

"That voice sounded familiar," Violet said. Jessie didn't understand why Violet suddenly looked scared. "I think it's Anna Argent's voice," Violet whispered. "She's following us! Let's catch up to the others!"

They hurried down. Jessie kept checking over her shoulder but she didn't see or hear anything else. When they got to the bottom, Grandfather was waiting for them. Jessie hurried everyone into the car and then told them about Violet recognizing Anna's voice.

Christina looked out the window as they drove off. "I don't see anyone coming down the path," she said. "Even if it were Anna, she'd have a hard time catching up with us now. Let's just enjoy the scenery on the way to Albuquerque."

"You're really going all the way around the world?" Henry asked. "That's very exciting."

"That's the plan," Christina said. "I'm eager to get out of the office and do something new. I'm a lawyer, so most of the time I help the Reddimus Society with legal matters. This trip will be quite a change for me." Her phone rang. She answered and then sighed. "All right. Let me know if there is an update."

"Is there a problem?" Grandfather asked.

A Sudden Change in Plans

Christina sighed again. "I hope it doesn't turn into a problem. The pilot has been delayed. I'm to wait at the airport until he arrives." She settled back in her seat.

"I have a question," Henry said to her. "What would you have done if we hadn't found you?" he asked. "How would you have gotten the turtle and the other items?"

"We had a backup plan." She smiled. "The Reddimus Society always has backup plans. I was to call your grandfather and arrange a meeting place. But you passed the test with flying colors. Mrs. Silverman is very pleased."

After that, everyone spent the rest of the trip

enjoying the scenery. Eventually they pulled into the parking lot of a small airport and went into the main building. A man came out of the office. Violet thought he might be a pilot because he wore a white shirt and a black tie with little silver airplanes on it. She liked that the tie almost matched his hair, which was curly black with little speckles of gray in it and cut short.

The man smiled at Christina and then at the Aldens. "I believe I have a friend of yours in my office. Watch, wake up!" he called. Watch came bounding out, wagging his tail happily when he saw them. Benny ran over and hugged the dog.

Christina said, "Hi, Jamal. Thanks for taking care of things for us. These are the Aldens. This is Mr. King, the manager here," she said to them.

"Hello," Mr. King said. "Watch has been doing a good job of keeping me company. We might need our own airport dog. Though if you want to leave Watch here, I'll be glad to keep him."

"No!" all the Aldens said at once.

The man laughed. "Okay, okay. I just thought I'd offer." He took Watch's leash out of his pocket and handed it to Benny. He took a piece of paper out of his other pocket. "Here's the address where you can pick up the dog crate for your flight," he said, giving the paper to Grandfather. "And your bags are over there." The bags were piled on top of a table in the corner.

While the others were talking, Henry and Jessie walked outside so they could get a better view of the airfield. There was only one plane on the tarmac, at the very far end near the last hangar. It was a gleaming white private jet with very long wings that turned up on the ends. Silver stripes on each side caught the sunlight so the plane almost glowed.

Everyone else came outside. "Is that the Reddimus plane?" Jessie asked. "It's incredible."

"It is," Christina said. "Would you like to take a closer look? You have quite a bit of time before you need to check in. And since my pilot has been delayed, I have plenty of time."

"Could we get a snack somewhere first?" Benny asked. "I'm really hungry."

Christina smiled. "We have some great snacks on board."

"I want to make sure there aren't any problems getting the crate," Grandfather said. "And I need to return the rental car, so I'm afraid I'm going to have to say no. We'll get something to eat at the Albuquerque airport, Benny."

Christina nodded and looked down at Benny. "Maybe another time," she told him.

Jamal spoke up. "Well, wait a minute. I'll be going over to the Albuquerque airport when my wife gets off work. That's half an hour from now." He looked at Grandfather. "You can return the rental car right now. Then the children can stay here to look at the plane for a little while. Then I can give them a ride over to join you at the big airport."

"That sounds like a good idea," Henry said, looking hopeful. "Could we stay here?" he asked.

Grandfather looked around at the children. He knew they wanted to see the plane. "Yes, if you are sure you don't mind, Mr. King," he said.

"No problem at all. I've got a few things I need to finish up inside."

"Wonderful." Grandfather checked his watch. "Why don't you children keep your luggage with you, since I've got Watch and my own bag. You can meet me at the check-in counter in about an hour."

Grandfather drove off while the children went inside to get their backpacks.

They came back out and walked toward the plane. As they drew closer, Henry whistled. "That is one sleek plane."

"I thought you'd like it," Christina told them. A man waved at them from the steps. "There's the copilot," she said.

There was a stack of boxes on the ground blocking the steps and a hatch open on the bottom of the plane.

"Sorry about that. Just step around them and up into our flying palace," the man said in a deep voice. He spoke in an accent they didn't recognize. They also didn't think he looked much like a typical pilot. His shaggy brown hair was long enough to stick out in funny angles from underneath his hat. He had a mustache that was shaggy too, but more black than brown. They couldn't see his eyes because he wore sunglasses. Even his sunglasses were a little odd. They were bright red plastic, and there was a tiny sticker of a yellow duck on one corner of one of the lenses.

Jessie stared at the man. There was something familiar about him.

"I've got to put the rest of the cargo away," he said. "I can answer any of your questions when I am done." He bounded down off the steps. Jessie still couldn't figure out where she had seen him before.

"Look!" Benny cried, grabbing Jessie's hand and tugging on it. "It's amazing in here."

Inside the plane were six large leather seats, three on each side of the plane. Each had a small screen mounted on the wall next to it. In front of the row of seats were a leather sofa and a table. Everything looked brand new.

"It's like a house inside a plane!" Violet said, sitting down on the sofa. "I wish we could go on the trip with you."

"It's very comfortable," Christina said, setting the duffle bag down on one of the seats. "The seats recline, so you can sleep in them. There is even a shower aboard next to the bathroom."

Benny tried each seat out, bouncing up and

down in them. Christina showed them all the features of the plane, including the galley and the storage areas. Jessie and Henry wanted to see the cockpit, but as they looked in, something outside the cockpit window caught their attention. It was Mr. King driving toward them in a red jeep.

"Has it been a half hour already?" Jessie said. She had hoped to be able to ask the copilot to tell them more about the cockpit.

"Who's that?" Henry said.

Another jeep, a black one, came speeding down the runway. It was going so fast, it was gaining quickly on Mr. King's vehicle. The person in the black jeep was wearing sunglasses, but as it drew closer, they could see it was a woman, her blond hair pulled back in a ponytail flying out behind her.

"Christina! You need to see this!" Jessie yelled.

Christina hurried in. She saw the jeep too. "It's Anna Argent!" she cried. "Stay here!" She turned and ran out of the cockpit.

"What's going on?" Henry asked. They looked out the cockpit windshield. Mr. King had just pulled up and Christina ran over to meet him. The

children couldn't hear her, but she gestured at the black jeep that was approaching him. Mr. King got out of his jeep and ran around to the passenger side and got in. Then Christina jumped in the driver's seat and turned the jeep around.

By now, Benny and Violet had come into the cockpit and were watching the strange chase. "Where are they going?" Benny asked. "Is she trying to escape from Anna Argent?" But they could all see that Christina and Mr. King were speeding *toward* Anna Argent's vehicle.

"She's going to crash right into her!" Violet cried out in horror.

But at the last second, Anna swerved out of the way then turned and went in the opposite direction.

Suddenly the copilot's voice came from behind them. "You'll have to leave the cockpit," he said. He didn't sound worried, but as they moved away and tried to see out one of the side windows, they heard a crackling sound and then a voice coming over the radio. The copilot shut the door of the cockpit, and they couldn't hear what was being said.

"Let's go outside to see what's happening," Jessie said. They climbed down the steps and saw that Christina and Mr. King were now driving after Anna's jeep. Suddenly Anna screeched to a stop near a fence by the airplane hangar.

Benny grabbed Jessie's hand, wondering what was going to happen next as Christina slowed down the red jeep and drew close to Anna's jeep. But something else was happening over by the airplane hangar. A man in a pilot's uniform came out of a side door. Henry was sure the man was going to go over to the jeeps, but instead he took off running toward the plane.

When he got close enough, they all recognized him. "It's Mr. Ganert!" Jessie said.

Mr. Ganert ran up the steps past them and into the plane, ignoring the children.

Was he flying the plane? Jessie wondered.

Henry shaded his eyes to get a better look at the jeeps parked by the distant fence. The red jeep was moving. "Christina's turning around," he said. "Maybe they're headed back."

But as the Aldens watched in astonishment,

A Sudden Change in Plans

Christina turned the jeep again and raced along the fence away from them. Once again, Anna and the black jeep were in pursuit. Both vehicles rounded the corner of the office building and disappeared out of sight.

The Aldens stood there for a few minutes in stunned silence, hoping Christina would return.

"What should we do?" Benny asked.

"You need to get back on the plane." A voice came from behind them. They hadn't noticed the copilot had come to the door. "There is a message for you."

The Aldens got back on the plane. The copilot shut the door behind them and hurried into the cockpit.

"What's the message?" Henry called out to him.

The plane's engines roared on. "What are you doing?" Jessie yelled. "We need to get off."

"Just take your seats!" the copilot called back.

"What do we do?" Violet said, clutching the armrests.

Henry's cell phone rang. "It's Grandfather on FaceTime."

When Grandfather's image appeared, Benny cried, "The Reddimus plane is about to take off. Are we...being kidnapped?"

"No, Benny," Grandfather said. He sounded as calm as always, which made Benny feel better. "I've spoken to Mrs. Silverton and Trudy. There has been a sudden change of plans. I think you'll like what's been decided. The Reddimus Society wants you to continue the mission and return all the items. Christina has something else she needs to undertake that's very, very important. I've agreed to let you go in her place."

Violet gasped. "That means going all the way around the world!"

"And that means keeping the items safe," Henry said as he realized what was happening. "It's a big responsibility."

"I know you can do it," Grandfather said. "And it'll be exciting. The Reddimus Society and I will be looking out for you every step of the way. You'll have help from people on every continent."

"Where are we going first?" Violet asked.

Just then they could hear the loudspeakers in

the airport where Grandfather was. "Flight 223 is now boarding," a voice said.

"Watch and I have to go now," Grandfather said. "Our plane is ready for boarding. Good-bye! We'll be in touch when you land."

Jessie turned the phone so that her sister and brothers could wave at Grandfather, and Grandfather turned the phone camera so they could wave good-bye to Watch too. Jessie sighed. She knew it would be too hard for a dog to come along on a trip around the world. "Bye, Watch. Bye, Grandfather," she said.

When the phone call ended, Henry and Jessie looked at each other, then at Violet and Benny. They all reached out and held hands, squeezing tightly.

Violet took a deep breath. "Isn't...isn't this amazing?" she said.

They all laughed.

The engines grew louder. The plane started down the runway then took off.

This is really happening! Jessie thought as she looked out and watched the airport grow smaller and smaller beneath them.

When the plane leveled off and was cruising above the clouds, the copilot came out of the cockpit. "Everyone okay?" he asked.

Jessie stared at him. He didn't have an accent anymore and his voice sounded very familiar. He took off his sunglasses.

"You're Emilio!" she cried.

The others stared at the copilot. "Where's your nose?" Benny asked.

Emilio laughed, reaching up to touch his nose. "It's still here. Oh, you mean the one I wore on the train?"

"Yes," Benny said, confused. "It was really big."

"It was, wasn't it? Just one of my disguises. People remember things that stand out about a person, so I like to add something that's not really me. It's easier to do my work for the Society that way." He took off his hat and then pulled on his hair. It came off too. "Wigs come in very handy," he said and reached for his mustache. He winced as he ripped that off as well. "I bet if someone asked you to describe your copilot, you would have said he had messy curly hair, a mustache, and strange sunglasses."

A Sudden Change in Plans

"You're right," Violet said. "That's all I noticed about you."

"You can settle in," Emilio said. "We've got a long flight. I'll tell you some airplane jokes on the way but first we have to figure out where we are going." He handed Jessie a small wrapped package. "A courier delivered this. It's a clue to our first destination."

The Aldens all looked at one another. "I'm scared," Violet said.

"Me too. But I'm excited at the same time," Jessie said. Henry and Benny nodded their heads in agreement.

Jessie ripped open the package. She pulled out a small statue of a cat made out of black stone. The cat sat upright on a stone base. It wore a collar of gold inset with blue and gold stones. The insides of its ears were painted gold.

"That's so pretty!" Violet cried.

"You'll have to put your heads together and figure out what it means," Emilio said. "And soon too, so we know where we are flying."

"We can figure this out, can't we?" Jessie asked, handing the statue to Henry.

"We can," Henry replied. Violet and Benny nodded their heads in agreement.

"Sure," Benny said. "But first can we have a snack?"

Turn the page to read
a sneak preview of

THE CLUE IN THE
PAPYRUS SCROLL

The second book of
the Boxcar Children
Great Adventure!

The Aldens continue their mission to return lost artifacts around the world by visiting the pyramids in Egypt and Stonehenge in England, but along the way they must outwit a thief!

The camels all sat in front of the stable, their legs tucked beneath them. All different colors of pom-poms and tassels decorated their bridles.

"They look like they are all dressed up to go to a party!" Violet said. "What's this tan one's name? Can I pet her?"

"Her name is Al Rahila and yes, you can pet her," Tareq said. "Benny, you and Violet can ride together on Al Sharif. He is old and a little slow, but good with children. Jessie, you can ride on Al Rahila. Al Mataya, the other tan one, would be good for Henry."

Once they were all seated, Tareq taught them the command to get the camels up.

"Whoa, we are really far off the ground," Benny said as he and Violet's camel lumbered up into a standing position. Benny was glad he was riding with Violet.

There was much more swaying back and forth in the saddle than from riding a horse. They rode near a small village and then past it farther into the desert. When they turned back and came within sight of the lodge, Tareq asked, "Would you like to go a little faster?"

"Yes!" Jessie said. Henry agreed.

The trip back to the stable didn't take long with the camels moving faster. Jessie had a bad moment where she nearly fell off, but she soon got used to the motion. At the stable, Tareq told them to hold on while the camels lowered themselves to the ground so they could get off.

"You are now camel riders," Tareq declared. "I'm going to feed the camels now, but if you are hungry, there is a buffet set up inside the lodge. Help yourself."

"Thank you for taking us on a ride," Jessie said. "Are you coming in to eat?"

"I'll be in soon, but I'll have to eat quickly. I'm taking some of our guests out for a nighttime ride to look at the stars."

They filled up on grilled meat kabobs and bean

dishes and a delicious Egyptian flatbread called *aish baladi*.

By the time they finished and headed back to their tent, Benny couldn't stop yawning.

Violet noticed and said, "I'm sleepy too."

Henry looked up at the sky. "I see why this place is named Desert Stars. Look at all of them up there. A camel ride at night to watch them would be fun."

"It's nice to be so far away from city lights," Violet said. The only lights they could see were those from the resort and from the village they had seen on their camel ride.

Benny walked into the tent. A motion in the corner caught his eye. It was a hand reaching through a cut in the canvas. The hand took hold of the duffel bag and dragged it through the cut.

"Someone is stealing our bag!" Benny yelled.

Jessie ran in behind Benny. He pointed to the corner. Jessie dashed over and tried to grab the bag. Her fingers closed on one corner, but whoever had hold of it yanked it through the opening.

Henry, who had come in too, yelled, "Outside!" and ran out the door. The rest of the Aldens followed.

At first, it was so dark, no one could see anything, and then Violet shouted, "There!" and pointed at a white shape darting behind another tent. The thief was wearing a long white robe, but there was so little light it was difficult to follow him.

They chased after him anyway, catching glimpses of white as they ran down the paths that wound around the tents. The person veered off toward the back of the resort, heading into the desert. Henry followed and managed to keep up, but he couldn't catch the thief.

Jessie had an idea. "I'm going to get Tareq!" she yelled at Henry. She turned and ran in the direction of the stable. Violet and Benny followed her.

Tareq was taking the saddle off a camel. He looked up, startled at their appearance.

"Tareq! Someone stole our bag!" Jessie yelled. "They ran out into the desert toward the village."

She pointed toward the lights in the distance. They could just make out a figure in a long white robe. Henry was just a dark shape running behind the figure, but Jessie thought he might be gaining on the person.

"Stop, thief!" Tareq yelled, but the thief didn't

stop. "No one steals anything from the Galal resort! We'll catch them!"

He jumped back on Al Shamlal.

"Jessie, take Al Rahila," he ordered, pointing at the camel Jessie had ridden earlier. "Benny and Violet, watch the others for me. Come on!"

Jessie barely had time to get on her camel before the animal got up and began to follow Tareq. Tareq urged his camel to go faster, and once it did, Jessie's camel sped up too. Jessie found herself clinging to the saddle so she wouldn't fall off. The camel was moving much faster than the jog they had done earlier in the day.

The camels drew closer to the running figure. "I'm going to try to get in front of him," Tareq called back over his shoulder. "He'll have to turn back then." Al Shamlal sped up even more, so Jessie's camel did too.

The two camels raced toward the village until they were between the village and the thief. The person turned to run the other way, but he tripped and fell just as Henry caught up to him.

As he fell, he bumped into Henry and Henry fell too. Jessie could see Henry grabbing for the bag as the camels drew closer.

Meet the Boxcar Children

HENRY ALDEN

At age fourteen, Henry is the oldest of the Alden kids. He likes to figure out how things work, which makes him good at repairing and building stuff! While he'll never brag, he's a great runner too! It's not always easy being the oldest and having so much responsibility, but there's nothing that Henry can't handle.

JESSIE ALDEN

Jessie is twelve and a natural leader. She's very organized—she makes lists in her notebook and always keeps track of facts when there's a mystery to be solved. When her younger siblings need help, Jessie's there. She loves planning adventures and taking care of Watch.

VIOLET ALDEN

Everyone knows ten-year-old Violet is creative—she loves to draw, take photos, and play the violin. She's a little on the shy side, but because she's quiet, she's a careful observer. With her artist's eye, Violet picks up on important details that her brothers and sister sometimes overlook.

BENNY ALDEN

Benny's only six, but just because he's the youngest Alden, it doesn't mean he can't help solve mysteries. He's always curious and full of questions. In fact, one of his favorite questions is "When's lunch?" because he's usually hungry! Benny loves playing with Watch and visiting new places.

WATCH

Watch is the family dog, a friendly and smart wire fox terrier. When the children lived in the boxcar in the woods, they found him as a stray. Since then, he has been loyal to the Aldens, especially Jessie, who once removed a thorn from his paw. Watch also has a special bond with Benny, who gives him treats!

Visit www.boxcarchildren.com/meet-the-boxcar-children to take the Boxcar Personality Quiz and find out which character is most like you!

Explore the All-New BoxcarChildren.com

Visit www.BoxcarChildren.com today, where you can join the fan club, ask the Boxcar Children a question, find out about new books and movies, download free activities, sign up to receive our newsletter, and much more!

The Boxcar Children Is Now a Feature-Length Film!

With an all-star cast including Academy Award–winner JK Simmons, Academy Award–nominee Martin Sheen, and up-and-coming actors Zachary Gordon, Joey King, Mackenzie Foy, and Jadon Sand.

Available on DVD or VOD from your favorite retailer!

Want to Add to Your Boxcar Children Collection?

Start with the Boxcar Children Bookshelf!
Includes the first twelve books, a bookmark with
complete title checklist, and a poster with activities.

978-0-8075-0855-8 · $59.99

And keep solving mysteries with new titles in the series added each year!

HC 978-0-8075-0705-6
PB 978-0-8075-0706-3

HC 978-0-8075-0711-7
PB 978-0-8075-0712-4

HC 978-0-8075-0718-6
PB 978-0-8075-0719-3

HC 978-0-8075-0721-6
PB 978-0-8075-0722-3

Hardcover $15.99 · Paperback $5.99

GERTRUDE CHANDLER WARNER discovered when she was teaching that many readers who like an exciting story could find no books that were both easy and fun to read. She decided to try to meet this need, and her first book, *The Boxcar Children*, quickly proved she had succeeded.

Miss Warner drew on her own experiences to write the mystery. As a child she spent hours watching trains go by on the tracks opposite her family home. She often dreamed about what it would be like to set up housekeeping in a caboose or freight car—the situation the Alden children find themselves in.

While the mystery element is central to each of Miss Warner's books, she never thought of them as strictly juvenile mysteries. She liked to stress the Aldens' independence and resourcefulness and their solid New England devotion to using up and making do. The Aldens go about most of their adventures with as little adult supervision as possible—something else that delights young readers.

Miss Warner lived in Putnam, Connecticut, until her death in 1979. During her lifetime, she received hundreds of letters from girls and boys telling her how much they liked her books.